SINK THE WARSPITE

SINK THE
WARSPITE

Duncan Harding

This first world edition published in Great Britain 2002 by
SEVERN HOUSE PUBLISHERS LTD of
9–15 High Street, Sutton, Surrey SM1 1DF.
This first world edition published in the USA 2002 by
SEVERN HOUSE PUBLISHERS INC of
595 Madison Avenue, New York, N.Y. 10022.

British Library Cataloguing in Publication Data

Harding, Duncan
    Sink the Warspite
    1. Warspite (Battleship)
    2. World War, 1939-1945 - Naval operations - British - Fiction
    3. War stories
    I. Title
    823.9'14 [F]

    ISBN 0-7278-5764-9

Typeset by Palimpsest Book Production Ltd.,
Polmont, Stirlingshire, Scotland.
Printed and bound in Great Britain by
MPG Books Ltd., Bodmin, Cornwall.

War's spite indeed and we do him right –
Will call the ship he fought in the *War's Spite*!

Queen Elizabeth I, in a play published in 1605

Author's Note

It is not every day, I suppose, that the postman delivers a package containing a large, left-handed hook through your front door. I can assure you that it comes as quite a surprise, especially when the razor-sharp hook is protected by a dried-out champagne cork of ancient vintage and you discover that there is a legend engraved in the silverbase of the substitute hand. In this particular case it read even more mystifyingly: 'Last remains of Lt. Commander Fergus O'Flynn, D.S.O., RN, Killed in Action, June 6, 1944.'

Why, I asked myself, was I being 'honoured' with the last remains of an unknown naval officer, presumably of Irish origin, killed on that magic Tuesday of D-Day over five decades before? When I'd recovered from the shock and placed the strange gift (if that was what it was) on the mantelpiece next to my latest Income Tax demand and a cheerful note from my publisher saying that my last year's epic was being remaindered at the enormous sum of 50p per copy, I rummaged in the wrapping paper to check if there was any clue to the provenance of the hook.

There was a brief note typed apparently on an old manual typewriter from a solicitor's firm in rural Devon, not far from Taunton. It read: 'Be so kind please as to acknowledge receipt of Hook (One) formerly in the possession of Lt. Commander F. O'Flynn', and added that the firm would be in touch with me in due course on behalf of a 'recently deceased client'.

I called the solicitor. He wasn't forthcoming. He was acting on behalf of 'a local gentleman, who was recently deceased'. He was merely carrying out instructions. However, he added in that thick Devonian accent of a group of southern Englishmen who seem to have all the time in the world, I could expect another package from the 'gentleman in question' in due course. And that was about all I could get out of him.

Naturally, by now my writer's imagination was running riot. A hook through the post; a further package on the way; a deceased gentleman, whose name the solicitor wouldn't tell me for some reason or other – why it was like one of those Victorian mysteries that had delighted me in my youth before I was corrupted by 'literature'. By God, Sir Conan Doyle would have flipped!

A week passed. No package. On the mantelpiece the 'left-handed hook' started to look a bit sinister, especially after a night out in the local pub with the 'boys' (not one of them younger than sixty-five). In the end, I hid it behind my prized bust of Winston Churchill. The Great Man, as everyone knows, had never been afraid of anything. Thus, I had forgotten about it when it arrived, addressed in one of those spidery, shaky old boy's hands that usually indicate that he's not far off snuffing it.

Again my imagination was stirred. Obviously the man who had originally addressed the package was the deceased client who had had the hook forwarded to me. Now he was certainly going to tell me why. With fingers that shook a little with excitement – and, it must be admitted, with the residue of the night before's ale (the old boys can really knock it back, but then they've been in training most of their lives) – I opened it.

My excitement mounted considerably when I spotted the name of the person who had originally deposited the hook with the solicitor for dispatch to me on his death. It was Jim

Hawkins! I could hardly believe the evidence of my own somewhat bloodshot eyes. Jim Hawkins! Hell's bells and buckets of blood – it was *Treasure Island* all over again!

The note that the dead Jim Hawkins had enclosed with the package of papers brought me down to earth once more, however. It started with the bald and decidedly unromantic statement: 'I have read a lot of your naval books, but if you don't mind my saying so, Mr Harding, I do think you make a lot of mistakes in them.'

I frowned. After that mysterious exciting hook and his name, 'Chief Petty Officer' (for that had been his rank), Jim Hawkins was going to be one of those bloody nit-pickers, who criticize writers for getting the Mark I quick-firing shit-slinger confused with the Mark II version. As if hack writers can afford to do extensive research on the kind of advances publishers pay them. Hell, a couple of 50p bus rides to the nearest reference library to check something and your advance is down the tubes.

But in the event, the dead Jim Hawkins turned out not to be a nit-picker after all. He went on in that dying man's scrawl to say that he was glad that somebody remembered 'us old matelots' and it was for that reason that he was going to give me 'the lowdown on the good old *Warspite*'. After all, Mr Harding, every other ship you have written about in your exciting books has been sunk. Not the *Warspite*. 'So what about tackling the tale of the "Old Lady", as we used to call her during the war?'

As soon as I had read a few pages of the handwritten text, I knew I was on to a winner. 'The Hawkins MS', as it is known at the Imperial War Museum where it now rests, was – and is – a beaut. An author couldn't have had a better story, and handed to him on a silver platter to boot. Naturally amateur writer-researcher Jim Hawkins, formerly Chief Gunner's Mate on board the *Warspite*, had made a few mistakes in all the years he had researched what had happened to his ship in World War Two. How could it be otherwise? He has spelled the name of that poor, crazy, fanatical Italo-German, who pitted his cunning against the great ship, in several different ways. Sometimes he is Breitmaier, then 'Breitmeyer'. Hawkins depicts him as speaking pretty fluent English as a prisoner on board the *Warspite* in 1941. Then as a POW in England three years later 'Mr B' speaks the kind of broken English usually attributed to Italian ice-cream sellers in the days when things were not so bloody politically correct as they are today. No matter. Nothing really could reflect on a story that just had to be told warts and all.

So here it is. The tale of Britain's greatest battleship in World War Two, the 'Old Lady' as two generations of British sailors called her, adding under their voices, when no senior officer was about, 'but by God could she lift her skirts sharpish whenever some foreign bugger tried to slip her a link'.

BOOK ONE

The Battle of Matapan
March 30, 1941

I don't think we can expect anything very dashing from the Italian Fleet.

Admiral A.B.C. Cunningham, March 1941

'Old ABC'* lowered his glasses. He was angry. Around the narrow bridge of HMS *Warspite*, his staff officers tensed. They knew the Commander-in-Chief was going to throw one of his feared tantrums any moment now. It was obvious Old ABC hadn't liked their advice. One of the Admiral's broadsides was on its way.

Old ABC took his time. To his front the horizon was growing darker swiftly. It was for that reason that the naval staff had advised against any instant attack. Night action was always tricky. It was filled with risks and uncertainties. Old ABC put his glasses on his chest. Still, he curled his boney, old-man's hands around the binoculars, and in the rapidly fading light the young officers could see the Admiral's knuckles were a bright white. He was trying hard to contain his inner rage. But they knew he wouldn't manage it. Old ABC never did. He had to get things off his chest. At heart, the Admiral was still the dashing, young, destroyer skipper he had been in the old war. Then he had tongue-lashed his subordinates into violent action. He still acted the same a quarter of a century on.

'Well,' he commenced with a growl. In the far distance, a faint light started to blink off and on. That would be the Italian destroyer-screen. But as yet, *Warspite*'s signals officer had reported no alarm signals from the Italian fleet. Mussolini's fine new navy, that was twenty years more modern than the veteran World War One British battlewagons, was ploughing steadily onwards into the trap

* Nickname of the Commander-in-Chief, Mediterranean, Admiral A.B.C. Cunningham.

that Old ABC had planned for them. 'That's the way of it, gentlemen, is it?' He flashed an angry glance from under his beetling eyebrows at the silent staff officers. 'You think I shouldn't attack. Too risky, what?'

No one responded to the challenge.

Old ABC had not expected them to do so. It didn't matter really. He had already made his own mind up before he had asked for their opinion. Still, it pleased the veteran Admiral to needle them a little. 'You know, you're a bunch of yellow-livered skunks.' He let the words sink in.

No reaction. Out on the horizon the signal lamp had been extinguished. The unseen Italians were probably getting ready to eat that garlic and spaghetti muck they fed upon, the Admiral told himself. It'd make them cream their skivvies quicker, once the *Warspite* and the rest of the British battlewagons opened fire on the wops.

'Right then,' the old Admiral said finally, 'I'll go and have my supper now and after supper, just you chaps see if my morale isn't higher than yours.' With a look of mock contempt on his old, worn face, Old ABC swept by them and disappeared into the interior of the great ship, leaving them to breathe a sigh of relief and tell themselves that it was always the same; Old ABC always asked for advice, but in the end he never took it . . .

Now the two great fleets were closing fast. Still unsuspecting, the Italian fleet ploughed on through the March sea at a leisurely pace, while the British cruiser squadron under Admiral Pridham-Wippell raced to reach the best battle position. Down in the *Warspite*'s radio room, the radio operators and detector specialists hunched over their apparatus, shoulders bent, hands pressed to their headsets, constantly fine-tuning the radios, tensed for the first indication that the Italians had spotted them. But they tensed in vain. The Eyeties were, it seemed, as Old ABC suspected, devoting their attention exclusively to the 'garlic and spaghetti muck' which he imagined they ate all the time when they weren't drinking Chianti.

At nine that March night, a signal came in from Admiral Pridham-Wippell. His leading cruisers were closing fast with an unknown ship which had stopped.

Old ABC reacted to the information like a man half his age. He thrust his false teeth back in – he always took them out to 'rest 'em' after he had eaten – dashed down a large glass of pink gin and darted up to the *Warspite*'s compass platform to investigate personally.

It was a dark night with no moon. A close approach under such conditions could be dangerous, he knew. He ordered the *Valiant* to approach the strange ship. She was the only vessel in the battle squadron with a radar set. Now he waited tensely for her to report. At ten she did so. She was only four miles from the ship. It hadn't spotted her. She was Italian all right!

Old ABC chuckled at the news. It was a strange sound at that time and place. A few of his staff officers said later, it had sent the shivers down their spines. It was like that of some ghoul in a Hollywood horror movie, gloating over the unsuspecting creatures who were soon to become its victims.

The Admiral was not concerned with such things. He had no imagination, well not of that kind. He ordered the destroyers in the screen to his front: 'Get the hell out of there.'

They needed no urging. Once the battlewagons opened up, they might well end up being slaughtered, just like the poor, unwitting Eyeties would be. They fled as slowly the heavy 15-inch guns of the three battlewagons swung round in a forty-degree angle and the decks of the great ships were thronged by sailors in their white flash headgears, so that they looked like many monks hurrying silently to their battle stations and their date with destiny.

Now, as the British ships closed with the still unaware Italians, Old ABC paced up and down the narrow bridge, always on the side facing the enemy. His tense staff officers waited. They knew the action. It was what they called his 'caged tiger act' and they knew, too, they'd be wiser to keep out of his way, save for the most urgent matters, as he waited for the action to commence.

Old ABC now handled his great ships like a squadron of destroyers, bringing them ever closer to the enemy, the only sounds his soft commands, the hum of the *Warspite*'s engines and the soft lap of the wash.

'Range three miles,' the report came through. 'See targets.' It was the Italian fleet's cruiser screen.

The old Admiral accepted the news with a curt nod. He showed no emotion, while all around him his officers felt their nerves tingling electrically, the palms of their hands suddenly damp with warm sweat. Most of them felt the urgent need to urinate.

'Ready.' The reports began coming in from the various turrets: 'Closed-up . . . Ready . . . Ready, ready, ready . . .' Time and time again.

Still there was no reaction from the Admiral. He continued to pace up and down on the port, wide of the narrow gallery. Then came the urgent boom of the fire gong.

'Guns,' they cried. 'They're going to open up.' Instinctively the staff officers stiffened their muscles and opened their mouths to prevent their eardrums from being shattered. Down below, anyone within the area of the main turrets fled. The blast from the 15-inch guns would swipe anyone in range from the deck as if he were a fly being swatted.

BOOM!

A tremendous flash. The night sky was split apart dramatically. The shattering concussion of three tons of high explosive shells searing into the darkness whipped the officers on the gallery across the face like a blow from a gigantic hand. Their heads snapped back. They gasped for breath like ancient asthmatics, the very air torn from their lungs, so that they felt for a moment they were choking to death.

Old ABC recovered first. 'That's the stuff to give the troops,' he cried to no one in particular. He whipped up his glasses. Up front, the destroyer *Greyhound* had switched on her searchlights. On her deck, crew members were firing flares into the sky. They exploded with a crack. The next moment, they illuminated the whole area with their unreal, glowing silver-ice light. The Admiral saw them. The enemy cruisers outlined a stark, harsh black against the light.

'*Zara* . . . and the *Fiume*.' Someone shouted out the identity of the modern Italian cruisers with their sleek lines.

Old ABC wasn't interested in identification. What caught his attention was the fact that the Eyeties had obviously been caught completely by surprise. Their guns were still trained fore and aft. 'Too much bloody spaghetti,' he cried with delight as yet another tremendous salvo thundered from the *Warspite*'s 15-inch cannon. Suddenly, suprisingly, the venerable old warrior danced a little jig of total delight on the narrow deck, crying out over and over again, 'Too much bloody spaghetti!'

Thus, to the aspect of an aged admiral, well into his sixties, dancing a crazy kind of jig while his staff officers, their faces outlined time and time again by the scarlet flashes of the *Warspite*'s guns, stared at the Commander-in-Chief in total disbelief, the Battle of Matapan commenced. It was midnight on March 28, 1941 that the World War One battlewagon, the successor of a line of Royal Navy ships which dated back to 1596, was going into action yet again . . .

*   *   *

'Hairless Harry' had been first to tackle the ship's name in his own ponderous Yorkshire fashion just as 'Chiefie' Higgins had been about to introduce the new draft of gunners to their duties in 'A' turret, back in Alex the year before. 'Funny name like, Chiefie,' he had opined while they stood in line in the hot sun facing the old CPO, who it was rumoured had served with Nelson on the *Victory* (though no one dare tell the petty officer that to his brick-red face; Higgins lacked a sense of humour).

'What's a funny name?' Higgins had growled in his thick Glaswegian accent, 'eh?'

'*Warspite*.' Hairless Harry had beamed at the CPO, obviously not spotting the danger signals in the CPO's red eyes. 'Can't make head nor tail of it, right proper I can't.'

Higgins had pursed his narrow lips and young Able Seaman Hawkins, watching the little scene that hot Egyptian morning, noted that old Chiefie was keeping his temper by an effort of sheer, naked willpower, as he grated: 'Funny how, Ramsbotham? Would yer like her to be called frigging HMS *Ramsbotham* or someat?'

Hairless Harry had grinned somewhat shamefaced at the use of his name and answered, 'Course not, Chiefie. But I mean to say, it ain't like *Nelson* or *Valiant* or *Queen Elizabeth*, is it now?'

Higgins had drawn in his breath sharply like a man sorely tried. But he caught himself just in time and said, 'Spite is from "despite".' He repeated the lesson that he had learned from another old chiefie back when he had been a callow lad like the bald-headed Yorkshire youth. 'Together with "war" it means a ship that doesn't give a two-penny fuck for anybody. Ain't yer seen that crest up yonder?' He indicated the battlewagon's official shield which depicted an ancient ship's gun, gold on a green field, and the motto, 'Belli dura despicio'. 'Can't yer frigging read?'

Hairless Harry had scratched his bald pate and answered, a little uncertain now, 'Course I can read, Chiefie. I got as far as Standard Eight in my council school. But that's in some foreign lingo.' He frowned.

Higgins, somehow or other, kept his temper. Perhaps he realized the big gormless Yorkshire sailor was genuinely trying to understand and not trying to take the piss out of him, as he always suspected new drafts were. He said, 'Well, that's Latin, me lad, and it means, "I despise the hardships of war". That's the kind of ship the old *Warspite* is and don't you frigging well forget it, matey, either, or you'll have old Chiefie Higgins down on yer like a ton o' frigging bricks. Got it?'

'Got it, Chiefie,' Hairless Harry had answered with unusual sharpness for him.

'Good, now shut yer bleeding cakehole and let's frigging get on with it . . .'

That little explanation had stuck in Able Seaman Hawkins' head, for it was the first time in that callow youth's life that he realized that he belonged to something very old and much more important and long-lasting than the shallow, petty world of pub, pictures and *palais de danse* that he had inhabited so far.

Now, one year later as the crew of 'A' turret, exhausted, black-faced with powder, burned here and there from the gun flashes, lay sprawled in the rays of the rising sun, Jim Hawkins remembered that day and realized anew that he did belong to something bigger and older than himself: something that, if he survived the war (and with the unreasoning confidence of youth, he knew he would), would make him proud for the rest of his life.

Wearily, CPO Higgins poured another bucket of cold seawater over Hairless Harry, who lay prostrate on the deck, a wet towel over his face, struck down by heat exhaustion. 'It's the frigging fans,' Higgins had cursed, as he and Hawkins had brought out the rest of the turret's crew after the ceasefire. 'They frigging well packed up on us agen. Yon *Warspite*'s warn out, laddie. You mark my words. Puir fond bugger that she is.' Despite his weariness, Hawkins had grinned. The Chiefie spoke about the ship as if she were a living thing.

Now he raised himself from the hot gun shield and stared out across the glare of the now calm Mediterranean to where the oily plume of smoke rose stiffly and slowly from where the Italian cruiser *Zara* was sinking. Behind him on the upper deck, Old ABC was supervising the raising of those triumphant signals announcing to the rest of the waiting British fleet that: 'General from C-in-C, Mediterranean. *Zara*, *Pola* and *Fiume* sunk.'

His handsome, young, unspoiled face revealed nothing. But inside, his mind was in a kind of turmoil: a confused mixture of pride, achievement and sadness at the thought of their opposite numbers, the Eyeties, dead and drowning somewhere near that pillar of funereal smoke. After all, they, too, were some mothers' sons.

'Penny for 'em?' It was Higgins. He had finished his self-appointed task. Now with his Woodbine concealed from the upper deck in the curve of his palm in the old matelot's fashion, he was having, as they phrased it, a fly spit and a draw.

'Just thinking, Chiefie,' Hawkins answered in the same subdued manner, as if it wasn't appropriate to talk too loudly with men dying only a mile or so away. He raised his voice a little. 'Never thought I'd see anything like this on a beautiful March morning.'

Higgins flipped his cigarette carefully over the side, though there were notices everywhere forbidding matelots to do so. But perhaps, for once, he didn't think regulations ought to be taken too seriously on this day of victory.

'Ay,' Higgins said ponderously, as if he were deep in

thought himself, before adding, 'you'll see more, me lad, before this war is out. I ken I was your age mesen when I stood on this same spot after we'd been hit by one of yon Hipper's ships at Jutland*. What a bluidy day that was. We'd been badly hurt. The turret was a frigging mess and the steering out of control. But I stood here all them years ago and looked at the scene, telling mesen I'd never seen anything like it and probably never would agen, if I survived . . .' He paused and the desire to explain seemed to have left him.

Hawkins didn't notice. His mind was suddenly racing after hearing the old petty officer's words. Higgins, as a youngster like himself, standing on this very same spot after another great battle, over a quarter of a century before. For a long moment he felt a sense of overwhelming awe. He, Jim Hawkins, had suddenly, he realized, become part of the *Warspite*'s history. More. He had become a small cog in the wheel of the whole of British naval history going back to the times of Queen Elizabeth herself – 'Good Queen Bess', as they had learned to call her in that council school which he had left only five years before.

But the awe-struck young sailor, bemused yet somehow elated at his discovery, had little time to ponder on it. For next to him CPO Higgins started suddenly. He dug his skinny elbow into Hawkins's side and demanded, 'Am I seeing things, laddie?'

Hawkins gasped with the sharp pain. 'Seeing what, Chiefie?'

'Over yonder to port . . . didn't ya see just then?'

Hawkins followed the direction of his gaze. For a moment he saw nothing strange, just what looked like an abandoned lifeboat from the *Zara* bobbing up and down in a flurry of sudden wavelets. Then there it was – a brilliant

* Admiral Hipper, commander of the German Heavy Cruiser Squadron at the Battle of Jutland in 1916.

white object hurtling through the sea, throwing up a bow-wave that increased in height with every second. 'Why—' he commenced, but the old Chiefie beat him to it.

'Holy Mary, Mother of God,' he exclaimed, 'a wop torpedo boat!' Next instant he had swung round, capped his hands around his mouth and was yelling hoarsely and urgently up at the bridge, 'Enemy craft off the port bow, sir . . . Coming in for the frigging attack!'

Breitmeyer laughed uproariously, as the wind cut his face, sending out his long blond hair in two wings behind him, carried away by the wild unreasoning speed of his frail white craft. The torpedo boat was going all out now. Way over fifty kilometres an hour. She hit each wave with her sharp up-raised prow as if it were a brick wall, great clouds of spray soaring into the sky, obscuring all to her front. On the deck, the gunners behind their quick-firer had strapped themselves to their cannon and were gasping and choking like men being strangled to death. At the bow, the torpedo mates balanced the best they could and crouched over their deadly tin fish.

Breitmeyer shook the spray from his gleaming, bright-red face and flashed a glance around his craft, satisfied with what he saw. He knew his sailors called him the 'Mad German' behind his broad back. But what matter? War was there to take risks – didn't he always tell his fellow daredevils of the 'Black Devils Torpedo Squadron' that it was their duty to 'fight like hell and make a handsome corpse'? Besides, he knew his sailors would follow him to hell and back. He gave the throttle a final twist. He had to get every last bit of power out of the mighty Fiat engines. Speed was of the essence he knew as he raced on, the impact of the bow on each wave shocking him to his very guts. He laughed again . . .

*   *   *

Almost immediately after Chiefie Higgins's cry of warning, the *Warspite* took up the challenge. She was a mighty ship, almost 30,000 tons of her. But once the damned little wop torpedo boat got beneath her main armament, she could plant a tin fish right up the old ship's arse and there'd be little she could do to stop herself being assaulted in this manner. The Eyetie had to be stopped while she was still within the range of the *Warspite*'s port guns.

Now it was, therefore, that the dawn sky was torn apart by the elemental fury of the *Warspite*'s guns at full blast. Huge spouts of crazy whirling white water flailed upwards. Surely Old ABC, watching the one-sided contest, felt that the pesky Eyetie couldn't survive such salvoes. But the blond giant at the controls of the speeding torpedo boat, spun her from side to side, as if she were a kid's toy.

Time and time again the torpedo boat seemed submerged by the spray of water. She reeled from port to starboard. At times her radio masts touched the sea's surface and angry, blue, electric sparks crackled up their length. But she survived, as if by magic.

'Hit that target . . . damn yer eyes!' Old ABC yelled to no one in particular, as the 'Chicago pianos', banked rows of multiple half-inch machine guns, thundered into frenetic activity down below. A solid white wall of blazing tracer erupted in the path of the bold attacker.

Breitmeyer laughed crazily. He was now being carried away by the wild, atavistic, unreasoning lust of battle. His blood boiled. Nothing was going to stop him. '*Avanti . . . avanti*', he bellowed, the words snatched from his teeth by the wind the very next moment. 'Die, Englishmen . . . die . . .'

Standing next to Higgins, watching this mad charge to death, Hawkins gasped, 'Christ Almighty, Chiefie, the Eyeties must have gone doolally.'

17

Higgins didn't respond. He couldn't. His trained eye saw that if the Eyetie didn't break to port or starboard in a minute, or the sweating, cursing machine-gunners didn't get the bugger, he'd smash full tilt into the side of the *Warspite*. Then, with at least two or three tons of high explosive torpedoes aboard the racing torpedo boat, the old *Warspite* would take a bloody bad knock – or worse. That thought vitalized him into angry energy. 'Come on, you lot of piss pansies,' he roared at the gunners ranged in their banks above his head, 'hit the sod, can't ye? KNOCK HER OUT OF THE FRIGGING WATER!'

Now Breitmeyer judged he and his crew were less than half a kilometre away from the old British warship. He knew that this was really the time to launch his tin fish, break off the action and, at top speed, race for the cover of what was left of the beaten Italian fleet. But that was not his style. He was going to push home the action until he was 100 per cent sure that he was going to sink the English bastards, who had so cruelly slaughtered the surprised Italian cruisers. Ignoring the shell fragments cutting the air all around the tiny bridge, and the huge waves of water from the exploding shells rocking his frail craft from side to side, he charged.

They raced on. All around him his boat was being ripped to pieces. The radio mast toppled down in an angry flurry of electric-blue sparks. Holes appeared as if by magic the length of the superstructure. The bridge shattered like matchwood. A shell splinter slashed the side of his face. But he didn't even notice. His whole attention was concentrated totally on the enemy ship. He blinked his salt-encrusted eyelashes. She seemed to fill the whole horizon now: masts, funnels, huge sixteen-inch turrets, the running sailors, even the oil patches on her worn old steel plates. The *Warspite* had become his whole world, his only reason for still being alive. He laughed out loud. But there was a note of crazy hysteria in that bold laugh. He squeezed the throttle with all his strength, trying to get every last drop of power out of the Fiat engines, crying, '*Porco di Madonna* – faster . . . in God's name . . . FASTER!'

A burst of 20mm shells slammed into the craft's wooden hull. She staggered, as if hit by some giant invisible fist. For one moment, he thought she was going to stop and sink. But luck was still on the side of the blond giant. The badly hurt craft seemed to shrug off the attack and then she was hurtling forward again, prow high in the air, rushing toward what had to be her final doom.

Hawkins's mouth fell open stupidly at the spectacle. He couldn't believe that they could be so brave – or foolish – as to challenge the *Warspite*'s tremendous barrage. The Eyeties were supposed to be yellow. But this boat wasn't. He was tackling a 30,000 ton British battleship, armed with massive 15-inch guns, with one fragile little wooden craft, carrying not much else but a peashooter. Yet the Eyeties were still coming on, smoke pouring from her damaged engines, reeling drunkenly back and forth as she was lashed time and time again by the shells exploding, surviving by magic that furious white wall of tracer and red-hot flak that was flying towards her. Hell's fire, how much longer could she last?

Breitmeyer summoned up the last of his strength. Blood trickling down the side of his face, he yelled, 'Discharge the kippers!' Usually the command was regarded by the men of the Black Devils squadron as a kind of in-joke. Not now. This was their last chance, Breitmeyer knew, to sink the damned English ship with his torpedoes.

The battered launch gave a great lurch. It was the torpedo slamming into the water, followed immediately by a wild flurry of bubbles as its engine commenced working. A moment later, the second 'kipper' followed. Now they were running towards the enormous bulk of the *Warspite*, trailing bubbles after them.

Breitmeyer caught his breath. Would they . . . could they? He held on to the heaving throttle, his muscles at the shoulder threatening to burst through the thin material of his torn tunic. In a minute he'd break. But he had to see 'Come on, come on—' he broke his own train of thought, crying in his soft Austrian German, '*Los, hau ihn einen runter!*'

But that wasn't to be.

Hairless Harry, recovered from his heatstroke, swung the 20mm Oerlikin around. He hardly aimed. Besides, at that range he couldn't really miss. He pulled the firing lever. The gun erupted. All around him the air was filled with the acrid stench of burnt cordite. The gun pounded against his big shoulder painfully. He didn't even notice. He was too intent on the kill.

The scream rang out. Shrill, hysterical, penetrating even the mad hammering of the quick-firers above. For one long awful moment, while instictively he waited for the burning pain to come, Breitmeyer wonderered who had given that terrible awesome scream. Next moment, a dozen red-hot pokers plunged deep into his soft flesh and he knew who. He had!

He fought back the hot vomit which threatened to choke him. He released his left hand from the controls. It was surprisingly covered with red dripping gore. With the grey veil of unconsciousness threatening to overcome him at any moment, he tried to reason why. Where had the hot blood come from? But try as he might he couldn't make it out. Nor could he understand why his shattered craft was losing speed by the instant and why there was icy seawater suddenly lapping about his ankles.

He raised his right arm to wipe away the blood. But he couldn't seem to free it from the control. It appeared to be stuck there. Then he saw why. The whole length of his upper arm was a mess of red through which the shattered bone glistened like pieces of polished ivory.

He felt he frowned, though in reality he didn't know for certain. 'It doesn't matter,' he gasped weakly, each word coming out in slow motion. He tried to exert pressure on the controls once more. He failed miserably. 'Got to keep going,' he hissed, facing up to that steel cliff which towered above him. He noted the red and winking white lights along its top. He couldn't quite understand what they signified. Below him, the shattered wreck was sinking rapidly. Why . . . ?

'Go on, you big gormless Yorkshire twat,' Higgins roared, crazed with rage, 'finish the wop bugger off! . . .What yer waiting for – a fucking written invite?'

Desperately Hairless Harry cleared away the stoppage. He gave a cry of triumph and pulled the 20mm cannon's firing bar in the same instant. The butt thudded against his shoulder. A hot blast slapped him in the face as he held on to the wildly chattering gun with all his strength. Great pieces of wood were ripped from the enemy boat. It seemed to be disintegrating before his very eyes. He yelled crazily. Next to him, Higgins and Hawkins did the same. Time was running out for the *Warspite*, they knew. If Hairless Harry didn't stop her now . . . they dared not think that particular thought to its logical end . . .

The last burst erupted just in front of the crazed blond giant. Bone splintered. His blood splattered the sinking deck in huge red steaming gobs. His ears filled with his own screams of agony, though he semed to feel no pain. Helplessly, his shattered body slammed to the deck, his bowels evacuating themselves with the shock of that terrible impact. Urine and excreta streamed down his legs. For one fleeting second he reached up an arm and tried to raise himself like a boxer refusing to go down for a count of ten. To no avail. A red mist started to overcome him and letting his arm fall weakly, he let it take him over.

He didn't hear the impact, as what was left of the torpedo boat smashed into the steel side of the *Warspite*, to crumple there in a mess of bent and twisted metal and shredded timber, scattering the dead on her decks like broken dolls cast carelessly aside by some wilful child.

For what seemed an eternity, those above stared down at that ship of dead; friend and foe clinging together like helpless lovers, screws churning wildly, purposelessly, faces numb and aghast, as if in total disbelief that this could be happening.

Then slowly, very slowly, the *Warspite* cast the launch aside. What was left of it, sinking more quickly now, taking its dead with it. The Battle of Matapan was over.

BOOK TWO

Rome, Alexandria, Crete
1941

Operation well carried out. There is no question that when the Old Lady lifts her skirts, she can run.

Admiral A.B.C. Cunningham to the Warspite

One

The leader, *Il Duce*, Benito Mussolini sat alone in his huge office, brooding. It was just dawn. Outside in the Roman capital, usually so noisy, there was little sound, save for those he associated with the city coming to life: the stamp of the sentries' boots on the cobbles, the rattle of horses and carts led by peasants bringing in their produce for Rome's markets, the jingle of the trams carrying the early morning shift to the factories. They were the familiar sounds that the Italian dictator had heard every morning in the eighteen long years that he had been in power in the country.

Today, however, they seemed strangely unreal. Everything did. By nature, Beniton Mussolini was not an imaginative man; imagination was fatal for politicians, he knew that. But this dawn, his imagination seemed to be running away with him. Everything appeared strange, different, changed, *ominous*!

Two hours before, when the servants had awakened him and in fearful hushed tones had told him what had happened off Cape Matapan, he had flown into one of those terrible, red-faced, furious rages they expected of him, sending them flying fearfully from his bedchamber once he had dismissed them.

Naked, save for a silken dressing gown which had revealed his bronzed muscular body in all its potency of which he was so inordinately proud, he had burst into the nearby bedroom of his young mistress, Clara Petacci. He had given her no time to awake. Instead, he had ripped the silken sheets from her plump nubile body, his sex already rampant and standing out in front of him like a policeman's truncheon, and had flung himself upon her, forcing her legs apart cruelly.

He had taken her silently, savagely, sadistically until she was thrashing and groaning and pleading with him to stop. He had not heeded her. He never did when his sexual pleasure was at stake. But in the end, soaked with sweat and panting as if he had just run a great race, he had risen, leaving her sprawled open-legged and glistening with perspiration on the rumpled, stained silken sheet, and returned to his office.

Behind him, she started to sob softly; why, he didn't know or care. He had to have a woman often when he was upset, as he was now. It calmed his nerves a little. What it did for the woman was not important. Women were there simply to serve men, especially when that man was Benito Mussolini, *Il Duce*, the master of what he called the 'New Romans'.

Now he brooded again on the defeat at Matapan. His Italian fleet, which he had vowed would dominate the *'Mare Nostrum'** in this new war against the supercilious, if decadent English milords, had suffered a bad blow. Two battleships had been damaged, three cruisers and a couple of destroyers sunk and his fleet had been forced to turn and scuttle to the nearest safe Italian harbour. What a feast day his many opponents in Italy would have when they heard about it, not to mention that drunken old plutocrat Churchill; he'd ensure that the whole world, especially America, would learn of Italy's shame.

Mussolini glowered at his unshaven image in the little

* 'Our Sea', as The Duce, Mussolini, had named the Mediterranean.

mirror he always kept on the top of his massive desk; it was useful for checking how effective his many poses were. Now his only hope to lessen the blow was that the *Regia Aeronautica*, the Royal Italian Air Force, had this night carried out its first successful raid against Churchill's capital, London. He stared at the ornate gold phone on his desk, willing it to ring and bring him the good news. Stubbornly the phone refused to do so.

For a moment he was distracted by the sound of muted cheering, followed by the tinny sound of an amateur band from outside. Puzzled, Mussolini rose from his chair and strode to the balcony from which he often addressed his New Romans. A small crowd had collected on the other side of the square, held by a group of self-important police-men carrying huge swords. Not that the crowd was very enthusiastic. Perhaps the police themselves had rounded them up from the morning shift workers to cheer the ranks of skinny boys in the fascist *Ballilla* organization who were now marching by, carrying dummy wooden rifles and commencing the German goose step with their skinny legs. Behind them came the white-clad girls of the *Piccole Italiane* and the boys of the *Giovani Italiani* youth movements. Automatically, Mussolini noted that the girls' blouses bulged with heavy breasts and told himself that they had the right kind of 'milk factories' in order to suckle his 'Sons of the Wolves'. Not that this particularly interested him. He had other and more personal uses for girls with large full breasts.

It was while he was watching a particularly attractive girl, whose breasts jiggled seductively beneath the thin artificial silk of her blouse, that the cavalcade of sleek black Mercedes cars came racing up the other side of the avenue, horns sounding noisily, drowning out the sound of the boys' band.

Mussolini flushed angrily as the lead car sped forward,

black-uniformed German SS men, arrogant and tough, hanging on to the sides. It braked to a halt. An SS officer, revolver already in his big paw, waved to the band to get out of the way. The playing faltered to a stop. Tamely the band and the 'Sons of the Wolves' behind joined the crowd of watchers. Haughtily the cavalcade moved on and disappeared around the corner, horns still going all out.

Mussolini's mood darkened as he returned to his desk. He realized that not only would this defeat at Matapan be taken up by his opponents in Italy and Churchill in London, but Hitler in Berlin would have to have his say, too. There seemed nothing that the Führer liked more than to criticize Italy and his handling of the war.

All the great hopes that he had cherished back in June 1940, when he had attacked a beaten France after the Germans had crushed the French Army in the north, had been dashed. His armies has failed in Greece and now they were failing in North Africa. His fleet had suffered a bad blow this very night and now, when the Führer expected him to join in the crusade against the Bolsheviks in Russia, due to start in a couple of months' time, his admirals were making a laughing stock of him and the valour of the New Romans. Soon, the German leader would be on the phone ranting in his usual manner, urging him to greater efforts, while all the while his underlying tone was one of contempt for what the *Tedeschi* scornfully called the 'Macaronis'. God in Heaven, what was he going to say to Hitler . . . ?

The rest of that morning passed in gloom. The Royal Italian Air Force had made a mess of its first raid on London. His airmen had failed, not only to drop any bombs on Churchill's roost, but they had lost eight bombers and five fighters without shooting down a single English plane. His reconnaissance planes in the Mediterranean had lost the departing British fleet and to top it all, the girl he had spotted with the big breasts marching outside had turned out to be a sour-faced young prude when he had invited her to his private apartment for *gelati* and *biscotti*. She had even had the audacity to slap his hand when it had wandered in the direction of those magnificent breasts of hers pressing through the material of her blouse, just asking to be fondled lovingly.

In the end, he had been forced to call in Clara, his mistress, who was still not dressed. But of course, foolish woman that she was, she had not understood his need. Instead she had pressed his balding, bronzed pate to her breasts, tears in her eyes, muttering *cara mia*, as if she was his damned *mamma* and had pressed one large dun nipple into his mouth. 'There . . . there,' she had said soothingly. 'Nothing can happen to you now, my baby.' God, what kind of treatment was that for a full-blooded Italian man, the 'New Caesar', as his admiring Romans called him?

But then the phone had rung and it was his adjutant telling him that the moment he had dreaded all morning had arrived. The Führer was on the scrambler from his home in Berchtesgaden. He wanted to speak to the Duce urgently. With a groan, Mussolini had released Clara's wet nipple from his thick lips and adjusting his flies had gone, dragging his feet like a reluctant schoolboy, to talk to the new master of Europe . . .

Urgently De la Penne focused his glasses. Around him his daredevils of the *Decima Flottiglia MAS* (10th MTB Flotilla) tensed. They were all used to risks, but these bronzed ultra-fit young sailors knew that what they were going to see now went beyond the normal risk of this elite and secret Italian unit. Over at the other side of the bay, sealed off at the moment by armed guards and police, the green signal rocket started to fall from the bright March sky. '*Attenzione!*' the man with the foghorn bellowed. The spectators needed no urging. They craned their necks forward excitedly, as the long shape, half-submerged and difficult to see even in the calm waters of the bay, came scudding forward, the two masked, rubber-suited figures astride the strange craft, barely visible.

De la Penne nodded his approval and said, 'Watch out for the nets!'

His listeners indicated they understood.

The craft, now visible as some kind of elongated torpedo as it moved, surged forward at nearly fifty kilometres an hour, heading straight for the submerged anti-submarine nets marked by little red flags. All of them knew that, under normal circumstances, the thick steel wire and hawsers which made up the net would stop even the most powerful submarine dead. Could this strange new secret weapon do the job for the MTBs which were now following, skidding gracefully with a comb of white water at their bows across the broad bay?

De la Penne tensed. He could see that it was time that his two guinea-pigs carried out their daring manoeuvre. If they fired now, they'd be too far off their target. If they waited a few seconds more, it was likely that they'd kill themselves with their new secret weapon. Silently he started to count off the seconds, checking his stop-watch as he did so. 'Seven,' he uttered, knowing that it was now or never – the line of red flags only metres (or so it seemed) away. 'Six—'

Even though he was expecting it, he was caught by surprise, as the two men fired their torpedo and in the same instant flung themselves over the side and started swimming furiously towards the speeding MTBs. He saw the flurry of bubbles. The torpedo was running true. It was heading straight for the little red flags indicating the presence of the submerged anti-torpedo net. He prepared himself for the detonation. It came. Suddenly, startlingly, the water in the middle of the line of red flags churned and twisted furiously. A second later, a huge mushroom of whirling seawater rushed skywards, almost blotting out his view.

The leading motor torpedo boat didn't hesitate. It kept on speeding towards that mushroom of water. For an instant, it vanished as it cut into it. De la Penne caught his breath. Would the boat survive? She did. Next moment she came sliding back into view, leaving the falling water behind her. She had cut through the net and, if this had been a real combat operation, De la Penne knew that the craft would be now swerving at top speed to deliver her deadly fish to her target.

All around him, the spectators had commenced cheering, with some of the ratings taking off their flat caps and flinging them into the morning air with joy. After months of trial and error, they had done it! Now there was no enemy harbour in the Med which was safe against this daring, dangerous tactic developed by the Black Devils of the *Decima Flottiglia MTB*.

De La Penne breathed out a sigh of relief. Out in the bay, the two brave guinea-pigs who had manned the human torpedo were being pulled aboard one of the following MTBs. He hated risking his volunteers' lives – they were too precious. But he had done so and it had been worth the risk. Now all he wanted was a target worthy of the risk he and his men would take if they were to put the manoeuvre to the test in some real combat situation. He wouldn't have long to wait . . .

The British surgeon-commander filled the long needle, sprayed a little of the drug and nodded to the sick-bay attendant. Obediently the rating carefully pulled back the sleeve of Breitmeyer's hospital pyjamas and dabbed the only free spot he could find on the pink, mottled arm of the prisoner with antiseptic. 'Ready, sir.'

The naval doctor gazed at the handsome young prisoner, whose burnt head still bore the heavy surgical bandages that they had bound round it in the *Warspite*'s sick-bay after they had rescued Breitmeyer from the burning, sinking wreck of his craft. 'I don't like doing this,' he said in careful Italian.

'You can speak English,' Breitmeyer said thickly, trying to fight off the pain.

'I understand.'

'Yes, of course,' the doctor said, trying to humour the prisoner; he knew well the excruciating pain he must be suffering. But still orders were orders and even senior doctors didn't disobey Old ABC. 'But it is a command from the top. They want to take you back to the *Warspite* . . . For questioning, I am told. The injection will ease your pain on the journey to Alex.'

Breitmeyer said nothing; he couldn't. The pain was too terrible. The whole left side of his bandaged, plastered body was flaming with it. Now he was grateful for the relief the needle might give him, though God knows why the English wanted him back at the great naval habour at Alexandria. Hadn't they interrogated him enough already?

He winced as the needle pierced bis taut, red-raw flesh. The surgeon commander said through gritted teeth, 'Just give it a minute. It won't take long before you get some relief.'

Breitmeyer held his breath. He waited, eyes filled with tears of pain. Outside his fellow Italian prisoners were playing a lack-lustre game of football in the sand with a battered, half-inflated old ball.

Gingerly, very gingerly, he started to let out his breath, prepared to tighten up his muscles immediately if the pain commenced once more. But it didn't. The shot the elegant, white-clad starched medic had given was beginning to work already. He gave a little sigh of relief. 'Thank you, Commander,' he said. 'That feels better.'

The medic grunted something and avoided the look in the prisoner's wet, red-rimmed eyes, as if for some reason he had a guilty conscience.

Five minutes later, he was in the back of an old box-like Army ambulance, with a guard armed with a fixed bayonet, squatting opposite him in the bakingly hot back, heading for Alexandria and the unknown, enjoying the relief from pain, but still wondering why the English had sent for him again. Had they found out about the Black Devils?

So *il Tedescho* lay wondering what the immediate future held, as he bounced his way along the rutted desert road to his appointment with the men he would later characterize bitterly as those 'damned perfidious English sadists'.

Seated on the battered wardroom sofa, the horsehair stuffing bulging out of it at spots, pink gin in his bony hand just like some ordinary sub-lieutenant, Old ABC listened to the merchant marine skipper describing the strange experience which had brought him and his naval intelligence staff to this urgent conference on the *Warspite*.

'I'd seen him early on, skimming over the waves like a beetle,' the old brick-red-faced skipper with the faded medals of the Old War on his dirty tunic explained. 'Well I thought I had. He was in and out like frigging Flynn – if you'll excuse my French, Admiral?'

Grandly Old ABC nodded he would and behind his back his staff officers smirked; Old ABC used more pungent, spicy language than that before breakfast.

'But then I knew I wasn't seeing things' – he finished his pink gin and the elegant aide, all gold braid and dangling lanyard, filled the skipper's glass up immediately – 'cos he attacked me with this mysterious thing.'

'Attacked?'

'Well, sir, this thing, it came hurtling across the sea –
I'd say more in the water than out of it. We trained the six-
pounder on it, but before we could lay the gun, the thing
had gone.'

Old ABC frowned and the lieutenant-commander of
intelligence, well aware that he had such a high-ranking
observer in the wardroom, snapped, 'How do you mean,
the . . . er . . . thing was gone?'

'What I said,' the old skipper said gruffly in a tone that
indicated he was taking no nonsense from these fancy staff
officers in their smart uniforms. 'Sudden-like she went up
in a sheet of flame and just disappeared.'

'And what did you do then, Captain?' Old ABC butted
in before the intelligence officer could react.

I hove to and had a shufti and searched around a bit for
wreckage or the like.'

'And did you find anything, Captain?'

'Nothing . . . well nothing to write home about, sir. 'Cept
this.' Like a a self-satisfied conjuror at a children's party
producing a rabbit out of his top hat to the gasp of surprise
of his audience, he produced from the battered Gladstone
bag on his lap what looked like a gas mask with an enlarged
headpiece. Old ABC peered at it with his old, but still
keen eyes, and noted the black devil emblem painted on
it, with a red trident in the devil's hand. He frowned and
was equally puzzled by both items, the strange mask and
the devil emblem, which evidently, due to the trident, had
some nautical significance.

The lieutenant commander of intelligence had spotted
the black devil figure too and he shot the old admiral
a glance. The latter nodded his understanding. He had
remembered, too, where he had last seen that same device.
It had been on the uniform shoulder of the big blond Italian
officer whom they had rescued from the wreckage of his

sinking craft before it had gone up in flames, taking the rest of his crew to their terrible deaths.

Now a silence fell over the wardroom, broken only by the cries of the deckhands, going about their duties patching up the battered old ship, and the Arabs in their bumboats plying their wares from the water of the anchorage. Old ABC gave a sudden shudder, like someone experiencing the first attack of malaria. The admiral's frown deepened as he was overcome by a sense of apprehension that he could not quite explain. Black devils . . . Eyeties showing heroism of a kind not normally associated with that race . . . strange craft surging through the water half-hidden by the waves at a tremendous rate . . . what did it all mean? Abruptly Old ABC knew with the certainty of a vision, that something was going to happen to the dear old *Warspite*, if he didn't do something about it soon. But what was it?

'They say there's a troop ship bound for the land we love . . . heavily laden with time-expired men . . . bless 'em all . . . bless 'em all . . . the long and short and the tall . . . You'll get no promotion this side of the ocean, so cheer up me lads, FUCK 'EM ALL!'

'Oh, put a bloody sock in it, laddies, for ferk's sake,' CPO Higgins moaned, his arm around the thick waist of the half-naked 'French' whore. 'This is supposed to be a frigging knocking shop, not a frigging choir school.'

Everywhere in the brothel's bar, thick with the pungent smoke of cheap Egyptian cigarettes and the fumes of even cheaper Egyptian rotgut *arak*, which the half-drunk matelots were tipping into the beer to give it more kick, there were cheers, wet raspberries and impossible anatomical suggestions directed at the red-faced old Chiefie.

It was now two months since the men of the *Warspite* had enjoyed a shore leave (even though the 'liberty' was only for a mere twelve hours) and with two months' back pay in their pockets, they were determined, as Hairless Harry had stated with a roguish grin on his broad Yorkshire face, 'I'm gonna get that heavy water off me chest reet smartish, mateys.' Hence they had picked the French brothel, and not the usual 'wog knocking shop' which impoverished matelots usually chose to get rid of their 'heavy water'.

As CPO Higgins had expressed it, 'Nothing's too good for the lads of the HMS *Warspite*. Why, them frog judies know more dirty tricks than you lot have had good dinners.'

Now, steadily becoming ever drunker, the 'A' turret gunners of Chiefie's team were preparing for the time when they were sufficiently high and without inhibitions and they were ready to go upstairs and take their pleasure. Though Jim Hawkins wasn't too impressed by the quality of these 'high-class tarts', as Higgins had described them after packeting a small fee from Madame Renée for having brought the *Warspite* matelots to what she called her establishment.

Most of them seemed old enough to be the young sailors' mothers. His was definitely well on the wrong side of forty. She wore high-heeled, laced-front boots of nineteenth-century vintage and her fat body was forced into a faded black satin corset, which tried to hold up her sagging breasts and failed lamentably. When she opened her mouth, which was usually to yawn, she revealed it was filled with gold teeth. As Hairless Harry had commented, 'Jim, if she goes down on yer with them choppers, you might come away richer than when yer went in. Look at all that frigging gold!'

CPO Higgins' 'girl' was no better though. According to the Chiefie, she had been 'personally' selected for him by the Madame. She was younger than the rest, but emaciated with a hacking cough and carried a black dog whip, which she cracked at regular intervals without any enthusiasm, breathing hoarsely as she did so, as if it took all her strength to do so. Still, Higgins didn't mind. For every now and again she stuck her wet tongue in his hairy ear and promised him untold delights once she'd gotten upstairs for a 'jig-jig'.

But on that March day in Alex, the turret crew were not fated to enjoy the emaciated charms of the girl with the whip or any other of Higgins' 'high-class frog hoors' for that matter. For it was just when 'Madame' had persuaded Higgins (and it had taken some persuasion with that canny Scot and plenty of the Madame's own personal attention to the area of his loins) to buy another round of 'cocktails', that they they were startled by the anti-aircraft fire, followed a few moments later by the dull thud of bombs exploding.

'Christ Almighty, heaven help a sailor on a night like this!' Higgins cried, 'what the frig's going on?'

Jim Hawkins, caught equally by surprise, got up so suddenly that the fat whore's slack breasts popped out of her black corset and hung there like two dripping white puddings. '*Sale con!*' she cried indignantly, as she tried to thrust them back furiously, 'what you do?'

But already the young gunner was at the window of the brothel and staring out at the anchorage stretched below in the slanting sunshine of the late afternoon, crying to the others in the room, 'It's the Ras el Tin lighthouse, lads. Somebody's dropping bombs on it . . . what the hell's going on?'

But the startled matelots and their squealing 'French hoors' had no answer ready for that particularly overwhelming question.

Two

'Commandante', the Duce had boomed over the scrambler phone, as if he were addressing one of his massive pre-war fascist party rallies, instead of a single officer. 'This is a matter of the utmost urgency, you understand?'

'*Si, Duce*,' De la Penne had answered promptly, not at all impressed by the upstart's style; after all he was a mere jumped-up former corporal of peasant stock and, like most Italian aristocrats, De la Penne, disliked the man. Still he was a patriotic Italian, eager to test out the new secret weapons being developed by the Black Devils and he knew instinctively that the Roman mountebank was offering him a chance now to do so. So he waited attentively.

'You know what happened yesterday at Matapan?'

'Yes, Duce,' he had answered, trying to make his voice neutral, though he still felt a sense of outrage at that terrible defeat of his beloved navy.

'Well, we must take our revenge immediately. *Capito*? There must be no hesitation. The English fleet must be struck – *hard* – at once.'

De la Penne had nodded his agreement at the phone but had made no comment. There was no need to. Mussolini would tell him what to do soon enough.

He was right. Mussolini had carried on in a great hurry. 'The English have returned to their base at Alexandria –

39

they feel safe there. Air reconnaissance shows that they are all at anchorage there, including their C-in-C's ship, the *Warspite*. You have heard of it?'

'I have, *Duce*,' he had replied, thinking that was a slight understatement. He and his Black Devils had studied the *Warspite* ever since 1940 when Italy had entered the war, looking for her weak spots – and there were many – so that his 'pig boats' could attack her quickly and effectively. But detail was wasted on the leader. Like all those show-off *fascisti* in their fancy black uniforms, they thought simply, in grand details. The hard precision work was left to lesser mortals like himself.

'Good,' the Duce had concluded. 'Herewith I promote you, De la Penne, to *Capitano di Corvetta* – and sink me this English ship, the *Warspite*.' With that the phone had gone dead in de la Penne's hand. It hadn't been unexpected. It was, as de la Penne knew, the Duce's grand military style. He felt Italians wasted words. They had to speak like the Germans – hard, harsh and brief. He smiled. But the Duce was hedging his bets with the bribe of promotion, all the same.

He and his men had gone to work with a will. Promotion didn't count in their calculations. They had swiftly toasted his new rank in a glass of *strega* and had then got down to the planning. The cover plan, the daylight bombing of certain points around the Alexanoria anchorage, had been worked out swiftly. 'We must make the English think we are retaliating for Matapan,' de la Penne had explained swiftly, as his excited young daredevils gathered around the huge map of the Egyptian naval port. 'The more haphazard it looks, the better. They'll think we've put the attack together at top speed in order to appease public opinion back home after our defeat.' His handsome aristocratic face had grown sombre momentarily at the thought of Matapan and then he had pushed on, telling himself that it was no use dwelling on the past. The future was what counted now.

So they'd concluded that once the English had stood down from the air attack and begun 'drinking that terrible piss-tea of theirs', as one of his officers had phrased it contemputously, 'they'd hit them with a full-scale night attack.'

As de la Penne had summed it up, 'Everything will depend on the accuracy of the submarine's plot when it brings in the pig boats. And the skill of you operators. The targets and courses will be prescribed. But each one should be prepared to change course if ordered to do so by the captain of the *Scire*.' He meant the submarine which would take them in and launch the top-secret pig boats and the two-man torpedo crews. He paused significantly and glanced around at their faces, as if seeing them for the first time and attempting to etch each and every one of their features on his mind's eye. Then he had smiled and cried, 'Orderly – more strega.'

Hastily the white-coated sailor had handed round glasses of the fiery cognac to the young darevils. Hurriedly, the newly promoted de la Penne had raised his glass high. 'Comrades of the Black Devil Squadron,' he had cried in a voice, now trembling with barely suppresed excitement, 'I give you a toast.'

As one, they raised their glasses and waited for their commander to speak. 'Death to the English!' he cried in his bold young voice. 'Death to the *Warspite*!'

In a firm bass they echoed the toast. In one gulp they emptied their glasses and without an order, they threw them into the corner where they shattered satisfactorily. The operation was on!

'Well,' Old ABC said carefully, nursing his glass of pink gin in his gnarled, bent fingers, 'he doesn't look much like a wop to me.' He pursed his lips and stared hard at the prisoner, who stood under guard at the far end of the captain's day cabin. 'More like a Hun.'

Breitmeyer returned his look, but the admiral didn't seem to notice; he might well have been talking about some animal or other.

The intelligence officer smiled. 'Oh he's an Italian all right, sir,' he said. 'Though he seems to have been born in the Bolzano region in the north of the country.'

The information meant nothing to Old ABC; nor was he interested. What concerned him was the fate of the fleet, in particular that of the *Warspite* in which he presently found himself. Outside, the fleet's ships' whistles were sounding the 'all clear', marking the end of the enemy air raid: one that had done little damage and had seemed to have had little purpose, as far as Old ABC could ascertain. He frowned. The thought caused him to remember why he had had the Eyetie prisoner brought here this evening. 'Tell him,' he said to the intelligence lieutenant commander who spoke Italian, 'that he is quite safe with us. He will come to no harm as long as he answers my questions. Clear?'

'Clear, sir,' the other officer said with more confidence than he felt. Breitmeyer, as he had already observed, looked a tough baby despite his injuries and obviously weakened condition. He turned and was about to translate the admiral's words when Breitmeyer said, 'It is no use. I shall say nothing.'

The intelligence officer showed his surprise – a bad move on his part. The prisoner's English was quite clear though it was heavily accented. 'Oh, you speak English,' he said foolishly.

Old ABC clicked his tongue like an irate old maid and said, 'All right, Lieutenant, you speak English. That makes things easier. Let me put the questions to you. We want to know what this Black Devils unit of yours is –' the

42

admiral flashed a look at the intelligence officer who had just provided him with the information – 'and what are the . . . er . . . pig boats?'

Breitmeyer's harshly handsome face was as set and severe as before and yet Old ABC felt he noticed a fleeting look of shock on the man's features at the mention of pig boats, whatever they damn well were.

'Well,' he urged, 'come on, Lieutenant, spit it out.'

Stubbornly Breitmeyer shook his head, lips clamped tightly together as if he did not trust himself to speak. Next to him, the intelligence officer felt a trace of sympathy for the prisoner. The man was in a hell of a physical state; he should not have been forced to answer questions. He ought to be in a hospital bed sleeping off his pain in a drugged sleep.

The admiral frowned. 'Do you mean to say that you are not going to answer my questions?' he rasped.

Under normal circumstances his staff officers would have smirked at the remark. Old ABC was like Jesus Christ walking across the water; he felt himself all-powerful. How could anyone have the audacity to challenge him? But not now. The situation was too grave. This mysterious pig boat business, whatever it was, was getting on all their nerves.

'No,' Breitmeyer managed to say, wincing with the pain of his burned limbs as he did so.

Old ABC didn't take long to consider his response. He made his decision and snapped, 'Very well, be it on your own head, Lieutenant.' He turned to the burly master-at-arms, standing rigidly to attention as if he were on parade. 'Chief, I want this man escorted below and placed under armed guard. You can handcuff him, if he gives you any trouble.' He looked at Breitmeyer to see if he had understood and added, when he saw that he had, 'If anything happens to the *Warspite*, Lieutenant, then it

43

will happen to you . . . Now, your last chance – what are these damned pig boats of yours?'

Breitmeyer bit his bottom lip to stop his mouth from trembling, but said nothing. Old ABC had had enough. Curtly, he snapped, 'All right, Chief, take him away – quick, get the stubborn sod out of my sight . . . I want to talk to my officers . . .'

Now the light had gone with the dramatic suddenness of the Mediterranean. To starboard of the almost silent fleet at anchor in Alexandria, a spectral sickle moon had risen. The clouds had parted and a curved slice hung over the sea, cold and unfeeling. Still, from the shore and the fleet itself searchlights flicked on and off at irregular intervals and swept the slick surface of the water with their icy fingers looking for something but no one knew quite what.

For even now, the staff of the British Mediterranean Fleet had not been able to find out any more information about these mysterious pig boats. Nor had Ultra in Britain been able to supply any more than their first signal indicating that they had picked up an urgent Enigma signal from the German ambassador in Rome to Hitler himself indicating that the Italians had developed a new and radical naval weapon to be used immediately against the British in retaliation for the defeat at Matapan.

So the staffs waited. Lookouts had been doubled. Gun crews had been placed on five minutes' notice and on shore, after the seemingly purposeless bombing raid of the after-noon, all leave had been cancelled and ack-ack had been manned immediately. As Hawkins commented to Hairless Harry down in their crowded stinking mess deck, 'Old lad, I think we're gonna be in for a bit of trouble this night.'

To which his friend had replied in that thick Barnsley accent of his, 'Well, if we are, let's hope yon Eyetie down below gets it up his nasty Eyetie ass first.'

Far below, his good arm chained cruelly by a handcuff
to the bulkhead, Breitmeyer, puffing hard at the Woodbine
which one of his guards had passed him when the CPO had
disappeared to the heads, knew only too well, what his fate
would be if the pigboats got within a striking distance of the
Warspite. He'd be first to die – or to drown slowly, fettered
as he was to the hull.

But Breitmeyer wasn't afraid, or if he was, his fear
was submerged by the unreasoning rage and hatred he
now felt for the English who had tethered him here like
some damned sacrificial goat. The young guard had indeed
slipped him a cigarette to soothe his nerves, but the rest had
been coldly efficient, pretending not to notice his suffering.
He felt it was typical of the smug, self-satisfied English,
who cared more for their damned dogs than they did for
their babies.

Suddenly, startlingly, he forgot his inner rage. He heard
it, he was sure. He cocked his head to one side to hear
better. There was the soft lap-lap of the wavelets against
the dripping hull. Had he been mistaken? No, there it was,
again. There was no mistaking that sound. It was the soft
chugging of a pig boat approaching at low speed. De la
Penne and his comrades of the Black Devils Squadron were
already within the anchorage!

De la Penne sighted the Ras el Tin lighthouse first. It was
some 500 metres away. They were, he was relieved to
note, dead on course and the English had still not sighted
the strange little boats, bobbing up and down on the slight
sea, waiting for his further instructions. They had reached
the net.

He caught his breath suddenly. On the pier there was
the flickering light of what seemed to be an oil lamp. He
strained his ears and thought he could hear voices speaking
in Arabic. Perhaps native watchmen. He waited. Around

him his men, their rubber-clad heads just above the water, did the same. Then the light vanished and once more they concentrated on looking for a gap in the net.

Once through, the drill was simple but dangerous. They would approach their targets, attach the magnetic mines to their hulls and then back off to salt the surrounding water with incendiary bombs. These were timed to go off one hour after the magnetic charges did. With a bit of luck they'd set the escaping oil from the targets' shattered hulls alight and turn everything into mass confusion. But first they had to get inside the net.

De la Penne ducked again. His men followed suit instinctively. Three craft were approaching the net slowly. He guessed they might be English destroyers. He could hear the thud of their engines at slow speed very close now. Could it be? It was. De la Penne and his men had come to the very spot where the net opened by sheer chance. One by one the English ships were filing through.

De la Penne didn't hesitate. He whispered to the other masked man astride the pig boat. He nodded his understanding. Slowly they started to follow the last destroyer. Behind them came the others. All that de la Penne could see of them were their heads and the very faint white wash thrown up by the pig boats' engines moving at slow speed. All the same, he knew a sudden mistake or suspicion and they would be surrounded by enemy searchlights, pinned down like ducks on a silver platter. He started to pray.

Slowly they followed in the wake of the last destroyer, bobbing up and down in the water, no longer visible to each other. All the same, the young daring *Capitano di Corvetta* knew they were following him; his brave men had done this often enough in training. He forgot them and concentrated on his front. Now, by straining his eyes, he could see the the old-fashioned square superstructures of the British fleet, a stark black, outlined by the icy light of the searchlights.

There they were. The *Queen Elizabeth* . . . the *Valiant* . . . the *Warspite* . . . He knew their silhouettes as well as he did that of their own Italian *Conte di Cavour*.

He frowned and started to steer towards the *Warspite*, the furthest away. The Duce had insisted that that ship should be his prime target. As he had stated over the phone in his usual bombastic tone, 'Strike for the head, de la Penne, their commander's flagship and the rest will just wither away when she is dead.' He wondered how true that statement was. The English weren't that easily defeated. Behind them the net closed. Now they had no choice but to go forward into the unknown. He concentrated on his target . . .

Breitmeyer held back his groan of pain with difficulty. Already he had bitten his bottom lip bloody with his attempts to stifle the agony in his chained-up arm. It was as if someone were striking a red-hot poker at regular intervals on the injured limb, with every new poke bringing him out in a lather of sweat. Indeed, the thin overalls the British had given him in the POW camp hospital were soaked through with perspiration.

Standing guard now in the gloom of the cavernous hull, the two young sailors, Hawkins and Hairless Harry, watched the prisoner miserably. They could see what he was going through, jerking every now and again when the pain struck him too hard.

Out of the side of his mouth, keeping his gaze on the lieutenant commander of intelligence, who sat on a chair and was twisting his head to left and right at periodic intervals, as if he were listening intently for something outside the hull, Hawkins whispered, 'D'yer think we should tell the officer, Hairless?'

'Tell him what?'

'Can't you see? His arm. There's a blackish sort of mark running up his arm now . . . the one that's tied up.'

Hairless Harry gave a little gasp and pushed his cap further back on his bald gleaming pate. 'Christ Almighty, you're right, old mate. That looks to me as if he's getting blood poisoning.'

'Maybe worse, Hairless. There's a funny pong I can smell coming from him.'

'You mean—'

'Yes,' his mate cut him short. 'They say when you get gangrene, it pongs like hell.'

For a moment the two young sailors, leaning there against the dripping bulkhead, fell silent, wondering what they should do, for it was obvious that the officer had not really noticed the prisoner's poor state. But how did a lower deck matelot approach an officer of the rank of lieutenant commander and tell him what he ought to do? Most dealings with the upper deck in the Royal Navy of 1941 were carried out through the offices of a petty officer. Officers were an exalted breed of their own; an ordinary seaman, even an able seaman, didn't approach an officer easily.

Breitmeyer moaned again and this time he made no attempt to stifle the sound.

The two sailors looked at him aghast. He really looked bad. His blond hair was matted to his skull with sweat and his mouth was hanging open and slack, with a dribble of saliva escaping from the left side. He looked as if he might collapse at any moment.

Jim Hawkins made up his mind. He was a determined young man, imbued with the decent English working man's sense of right and wrong; what he would have called fair play. He cleared his throat and said in a dry voice that he hardly recognized as his own, 'Sir.'

The intelligence officer turned and stared at him puzzled. Finally he said, 'Yes?'

'It's the prisoner, sir.'

'What about him?'

Jim Hawkins flushed a deep red. 'Begging yer pardon, sir. But he don't look too hot to me, sir . . . and you can see there's a nasty red mark running down his left arm. That looks like poisoning or something to me, sir.' He stopped abruptly, as if he felt he had said enough.

The lieutenant commander stared at Breitmeyer. For a long moment he said nothing. Then he remarked, 'You're right, seaman. That arm was in bad shape as it was. Now tied up like that the blood isn't circulating.'

'Can't you do anything, sir?' Hairless Harry asked, using his best English. 'The sod looks as if he could snuff it at any moment.'

The officer acted. He strode over to the wall phone and snapped, 'Bridge.'

Breitmeyer didn't seem to notice. His head hung down, one arm raised like some latterday Christ on the Cross.

The phone buzzed. 'C-in-C, please.' The lieutenant commander straightened himself up automatically, as if he might spring to attention once the commander-in-chief responded.

Hurriedly he explained the position to Old ABC, adding, 'I think he needs urgent medical attention, sir. He looks bad and his arm, too.' His face fell. Obviously the C-in-C wasn't pleased with his request. He stammered, 'I just thought I ought to report the situat—' He stopped abruptly. The phone had gone dead. Slowly, very slowly, he replaced it. 'Sorry, lads,' he said, 'the C-in-C won't buy it. Either the prisoner talks or he stays here till . . .' He didn't tell them what the C-in-C had said should happen then, but it wasn't pleasant and they knew it.

Hairless Harry looked at the officer, then at the motionless prisoner and finally at Hawkins. His look said everything. The prisoner was staying here, tied up, arm or no arm.

Hairless Harry shrugged.

Jim Hawkins did the same. He didn't like it, but there was nothing he could do about it. Against the bulkhead *Tenente* Breitmeyer groaned once more. But the pain was lessening now. The reason was simple. His left arm was beginning to die . . .

Gingerly de la Penne nosed his ugly craft, which had given it the name of pig boat in the Black Devils Squadron, towards the *Warspite*, which towered above them like a gigantic sheer steel cliff. He could just make out the riding lights high above him. But so far the English didn't seem aware of the danger they were in.

Behind him his crewmate reduced speed to almost nothing, but just sufficient to be able to fight the tide and keep the pig boat on course. All about him the rest of the squadron edged their way to their targets, one of them heading for a large fleet oil tanker, which lay fat and heavy in the water, filled with fuel. It would burn like an inferno once the mine went off, de la Penne told himself, and then dismissing the other pig boat he concentrated on the difficult business of anchoring himself to the *Warspite*'s hull.

With the cold creeping inside his rubber suit after several hours of immersion since leaving the submarine, he found it exceedingly difficult to loosen the screws which fixed the explosive charges to the pig boat. Gritting his teeth, his hands numb and unfeeling, as if they were enclosed in thick boxing gloves, he undid them one by one until, gasping hard, he'd done it. He took a deep breath and whispered, 'Get ready to cast off.' Slowly, very slowly, he pushed the charge towards the *Warspite*.

The powerful magnets took over. They almost tore the high explosive capsule from his nerveless fingers. Before he could slow down the process, the charges were ripped loose and with a resounding clank that de la Penne thought could be heard all over the Alexandria anchorage, they slammed against the hull. De la Penne caught his breath. Now he was for it . . . Nothing. Seemingly the noise had gone unnoticed.

Then trouble struck from an unexpected quarter. Without warning, the rest of the pig boat, relieved of its heavy charge, sank beneath him, taking the second pilot with it. One moment de la Penne had a firm base under his frozen feet, the next it had vanished and he found himself treading water furiously, consuming oxygen from his oxygen cylinder at an alarming rate. '*Porco di Madonna*,' he commenced frantically. Then he caught himself in time. He must not panic; he'd use up the oxygen he'd need to swim to safety if he could not find the rest of the pig boat. He made himself count slowly to three and then with the spoken command 'now' he squirmed round and dived.

'Well, damn it,' Old ABC growled to his chief-of-staff, putting down his third pink gin of the last hour, 'anything to report?'

'Yes, Admiral,' the other officer replied. 'We know what a pig boat is now.'

Old ABC sat up with sudden speed for such an old man. 'You what?' he exclaimed.

'Yes, sir. We've nabbed one. The *Valiant* spotted it and winched it aboard. Your guess was right, sir. It's an explosive charge, worked by magnets and delayed fuse – rather like a limpet mine – attached to a sort of underwater large-sized torpedo with a motor powering it. The mine's attached and what's left of this pig boat pulls away with the two operators to safety before the balloon goes up.'

Old ABC swallowed the rest of his gin in a rapid gulp. 'Damned cunning buggers, these wops,' he snorted thickly.

'Always said so.' He controlled his outrage: 'Go on, old chap. Prisoners?'

'Unfortunately not, sir. We think the two operatives swam ashore. Naturally we'll pick 'em up in due course, but not at the moment . . .' The words died on the chief-of-staff's lips. He could see that the boss was thinking.

He was right. Old ABC now reasoned that the way the Italians were operating was to attach their damned magnetic mines below the waterline and especially below the bulge of extra armour which gave the battlewagons protection against enemy torpedoes. So he had been right in placing their Black Devils prisoner in the bottom of the hull. If anyone was going to hear the placing of a limpet mine, it would be him, and if he wanted to save his wop skin, he'd be first to shout out a warning. The only thing was that the stubborn bugger was refusing to co-operate. He made up his mind. 'Tell intelligence to put the pressure on that wop prisoner. Tell him we know all about their damned pig boats and he's going to be the first victim, if he doesn't shout up as soon as he hears anything.'

'But his arm, sir—'

'Bugger his arm!' the C-in-C interrupted harshly. 'My ships and my crews are more important to me than some bloody greaser's left arm. Then get the divers down at every ship . . . in double teams. Anyone capable of diving is to be sent down. Forget the risks. It's max effort. Now get to it.'

The hunt was on. Now it was the might of the British Royal Navy pitted against a handful of brave, if suicidal Italian divers . . .

Bruno, his co-pilot, was dead. De La Penne saw that straightaway. A loose hawser from the *Warspite* had curled itself around his neck and strangled him to death. Now he stood there swaying and wavering in the moving sea, hands stuck against the cable that had killed him so treacherously, as if for eternity. Not far away was the craft, engine dead.

De la Penne made a swift decision. He wouldn't attempt to restart the engine. That might give the game away. He'd swim for it, heading for the Ras el Tin lighthouse. There was still a sizeable Italian community in Alexandria. With luck, if he made the shore, some fascist sympathizer might hide him till he could make a plan to reach his compatriots in the Western Desert. His mind made up, he started upwards once more.

He broke the surface. Gasping for breath and treading water, he turned a full 360 degree circle. There was more activity than before and he guessed the English had been alerted. Every now and again someone blew an alarm whistle and searchlights were sweeping the anchorage. Oh yes, the Tommies were on the alert all right. But, de la Penne told himself, sometimes situations of confusion were the best for any escaper. He decided he had a chance. He set off for the lighthouse, trying to force himself to take his time and conserve energy, only to find himself swimming hard and panting frantically with the effort.

Now he was weaving in and out of smaller ships. He guessed he was getting to more shallow water. He was making it. Suddenly he felt renewed hope. He was going to make it. Soon the bombs would start exploding, but by that time, with a bit of luck, he'd be ashore near the lighthouse.

But that wasn't to be. There was the first hollow boom of a magnetic charge going off. Later de la Penne thought it was the one attached to the *Queen Elizabeth*. Next moment the blast set the water all around him swaying angrily back and forth, knocking the air from his lungs, so that in an instant he was frighteningly gasping and choking for breath.

Next moment, all hell broke loose and de la Penne, with the certain of a sudden vision, knew all was lost. He'd never make it now.

Far to the right, there was a tremendous roar. The scarlet flash of a mine exploding split the darkness. White gleaming metal splinters zig-gagged crazily into the air. Next moment the incendiaries, which the pig boat pilots had laid, went off in a shower of fiery-white sparks. In a flash, the sea started to blaze all around the *Valiant*.

Sirens shrieked; bosuns shrilled their whistles; ratings swung their alarm rattles; men ran back and forth; fire parties broke out their hoses and water jets flew back and forth. In an instant all was controlled chaos. Up on the bridge of the *Warspite*, rocked now by an explosion of its own, Old ABC opened his mouth wide to prevent his eardrums from being burst by the explosion. A moment later, a shock wave hit his old wrinkled face like a blow from a damp, flabby open hand. For an instant, he glimpsed what looked like an oversized torpedo flying crazily through the burning red sky, and knew he had caught his first sight of a pig boat. Next second, all was pitch black and he was blinking his eyes rapidly, telling himself that the *Warspite* had been hit, but that she would survive. She always would, the old ship. After all, wasn't her ancient motto *Belli dura despicio* – I despise the hardships of war?

Three

It was 'Slops'.

Hawkins and Hairless Harry lounged against the *Warspite*, enjoying the May sunshine, while the matelots lined up in the various queues that always occurred at the fortnightly slops. There were men ready to pick up their pay in their best caps. Others were waiting for the tailors to arrive, or 'jewing' firms as they were called. They were amateur tailors, who were expert all the same in producing the skintight bell-bottoms that young sailors loved, and which seemed to make the sailors' feet disappear so that they seemed to be floating footless above the ground when they moved. Then there was the tobacco issue: half-pound tins of leaf tobacco which the sailors rolled into gaspers or 'coffin nails' themselves, or if they were 'old heads' turned into 'pricks' of pipe tobacco.

But at this particular slops, the two young sailors were more interested in the never-ending chain of supplies being offloaded on the C-in-C's flagship; they were experienced enough now to know that the kind and quantity of supplies might give them a clue as to where the ship might be sailing and for how long.

They had already noted that a thousand gallons of rum had been taken aboard and about twenty tons of fresh meat and fish. Now, as they lounged there with apparently not a care in the world, enjoying this short time out of war, they observed ton after ton of tinned

55

and dried provisions following the fresh goods, which finally occasioned Hairless to whisper in that thick South Yorkshire accent of his, 'Mate, I don't think we're gonna touch many friendly ports wherever we're off to.'

Hawkins nodded his agreement. He had come to the same conclusion. In peacetime, ships like the *Warspite*, the pride of the Royal Navy, never ran out of fresh food. In wartime it was different. When the ship did run out, it either bought supplies in friendly ports, or if they weren't available, the matelots had to buckle down and go on to tinned meat and vegetables.

Hawkins stubbed out the last of his hand-rolled 'ticklers', before he could purchase any more duty-free and said, 'Where do you think we're off to then, Hairless?'

The other sailor shrugged and grunted, 'Who do yer think I am, matey, Jesus Christ?' His tone changed: 'Well, you can bet yer bottom dollar, Jim, if it's in the Med, there's nothing between Alex and Gib where we can run in for supplies. Malta's out, that's for sure.'

'Yes, I don't fancy the Grand Harbour at Valetta either. The Jerries and the Eyeties are knocking the living bloody daylights out of it.'

Hairless sniffed and nodded over to where the line for the duty-free tobacco had begun to shuffle forward, while the 'tickler firms', the matelots who made it up into cigarettes or ticklers for a small fee, started shouting their prices, trying to underbid each other in farthings. 'Come on, Jim, better get in line.'

But on that particular slops day, the two gunners weren't fated to pick up their tins of Capstan Navy Cut and the like, for just when they were about to join the queue, CPO Higgins appeared from nowhere, little eyes gleaming redly as if he had already been at his neat rum ration tot for this day, and snapped, 'Hey, you two, where are you buggering off to, may I ask?'

'It's Slops, Chiefie,' Hairless said slow and loud as if he were explaining to some aged deaf crone. 'We're gonna pick up our tobacco ration.'

Higgins glared at him with those bloodshot eyes of his and snarled, 'Yer gonna pick up the end of me boot up that big Yorkshire arse of yourn if you give me any more of yon dumb insolence, yer ken. I'm not deaf, yer bald bugger.'

Hairless Harry flushed. He was very sensitive about his hair, or the lack of it – he spent a fortune on bay rum in the hope that it might restore his vanished locks. Hurriedly, Jim Hawkins stepped in and said, 'Where's the fire, Chiefie? What's up?'

The old petty officer with the gold crossed cannon of his rank on his 'Number One suit' lowered his voice: 'I've just heard a buzz in the petty officers' mess when I was having . . . er . . . a cup of tea.' He lied glibly without even a blush, breathing rum fumes all over the two young sailors. 'The balloon's gone up over Crete.'

'Crete?'

'Yes, the Jerries are dropping airborne troops according to the buzz. Naturally they'll be followed by seaborne Jerry troops – and we're off to stop 'em!'

The two young sailors looked at each other and Hawkins said, 'Looks dicey, Chiefie . . . without air cover.'

'Maybe,' was all that the old veteran petty officer would concede. 'But when hasn't the situation bin dicey for the *Warspite*?' He tugged the end of his red pitted nose and licked his lips, as if they were suddenly very dry. 'She'll make it all right – she allus does. Now, you two, I'm off to get some office work done. Meanwhile, you two can sling yer hooks from here and get back to "A" turret and see what's going on.'

With that he was gone, obviously heading for another glass of the neat rum that was allotted only to petty officers, while the ordinary seamen were given grog – rum well watered down. The two watched him go with his Scottish bow-legged shuffle. At any other time, Jim Hawkins would have made a comment at the old chiefie's haste to get back to his rum, but not now; he was too worried. So he contented himself with: 'What a turn-up for the book, Hairless.' Then, when his shipmate didn't react, he slung his hook without another word . . .

May 21, 1941

All the previous day, the *Warspite* and the flotilla of destroyers under the command of Captain Lord Mountbatten* had been sailing off the Greek island, bombarding the new German positions. The German *Fallschirmjagers* had come down in their hundreds, perhaps thousands, being riddled by the New Zealand and British infantry below, shot in their chutes like tame game birds. All the same, despite their horrendous casualties, the German paras had managed to dig in here and there and establish defended positions for the follow-up troops; and as a sweating, red-faced CPO Higgins snorted angrily, 'Ye dinna need a frigging crystal ball to know they'll bring up reinforcements by water from the Greek mainland!'

Now, on this second day of the great German airborne invasion, the Germans brought the overwhelming strength of their mainland-based Luftwaffe into play, and from dawn onwards, the sky above the British force was peppered by the black puffballs of smoke, as the ship's flak tried to ward off the German dive-bombing attacks.

Time and time again, squadrons of enemy Stuka divebombers, looking like sinister black metallic hawks, arrived over the handful of British ships and hovered there apparently motionless. Then with sudden, startling speed, the

---

* See D. Harding: *Sink the Kelly* (Severn House) for further details.

leader would fall out of the blue sky, sirens screaming, commencing that death-defying dive of the Stuka pilot. Down and down the leader would come hurtling, as if nothing could stop it from plunging to his destruction in the sea below, flame and smoke from the flak exploding on both sides. Then, at the very last moment when it appeared catastrophe could not be avoided, the pilot would level out. A myriad of deadly little eggs would emerge from its blue-painted belly and in a crazy flash, the water all around the *Warspite* would erupt into a maelstrom of crazy water and sudden death.

Somehow the men on the bridge, handling the great 30,000 ton battleship like a lean lithe destroyer, managed to avoid the bombs time and time again. But even the most optimistic of the ship's crew knew that the *Warspite*'s luck couldn't hold out for ever.

It didn't.

Just after midday when the crew, during a pause in the battle, had gulped down a hurried meal of corned beef sandwiches and luke-warm cocoa (for most of the galley fires had been blown out by the firing), the Germans pulled a new trick on the hard-pressed defenders. Suddenly, frighteningly, four Me 109 fighter-bombers appeared out of nowhere. They came zooming in at mast height in line, abreast, heading straight for the *Warspite* out of the smoke of battle.

It was clear what their target was. Not the destroyers or the light cruisers. It was the *Warspite* itself. And they had caught the ack-ack gunners completely off guard. Frantically, the gunners manning the deck machine guns and banked Chicago pianos took up the challenge. A solid wall of white tracer erupted in front of the Messerschmitts. One staggered in mid-air. It was as if the plane had just run into an invisible wall. A ragged cheer went up from the defenders. It was premature. The German plane shook and then, with black smoke trailing from its fuselage, it came on with the rest.

'Full to port!' the captain on the bridge yelled frantically, as the attackers flew ever closer, zooming effortlessly through the blazing white network of ack-ack fire.

The helmsman responded immediately. The great ship, shaking and trembling under the strain, answered the command, swinging round. Too late. The attackers were already dropping their lethal 300-pound armour-piercing bombs. Two bombs fell to either side of the great ship. She reeled as if she had been punched by some gigantic fist. In 'A' turret, CPO Higgins's gunners held on for their very lives. Instruments shattered. Plates burst. Water started to trickle in at a dozen different points. But still the *Warspite* continued on her course. But only for a few moments.

Next instant the whole ship seemed to quiver and leap out of the water as a 500-pound bomb skidded into the starboard side of the forecastle deck. It exploded with devastating effect. A great wind swept the length of the *Warspite*. Screaming, crazed ratings were carried over the side. Boats splintered like matchwood. A mast came tumbling down in a shower of blue-and-red angry sparks. In an instant, all was chaos and confusion and it was clear that the great old ship had been badly hurt.

Not only had the forecastle deck been penetrated and a 4-inch gun turret on that deck wiped out completely, but a dangerous fire had started in the starboard battery and all the ship's 6-inch guns had been knocked out of action. In essence, the ship's major anti-aircraft defences had been destroyed, while below decks a boiler room had been so badly hit that it had to be abandoned. The ship was in such a bad way that the admiral, Admiral Rawlings, who had taken over from Old ABC, who was now in Alexandria, remarked quietly to the captain, 'Well, old chap, I wonder which dockyard in America will take you to repair this bugger?'

The captain merely smiled. He wondered at that moment if they'd ever reach the USA.

Down below from the bridge, as the attackers flew off into the smoke, the fire control parties, the rescue teams and the sick-bay attendants swarmed out to clear the decks the best they could before the next attack came – and the *Warspite*'s senior officers were pretty certain that wouldn't be long. Once the Germans scented a 'kill', they never let up.

The various teams were met by scenes of terrible carnage. There were dead and dying everywhere, piled up in the grotesque positions of those who had died violently. Men had been ripped apart by the steel fragments which had flown everywhere, shredded their flesh so that their bones glistened like polished ivory in the midst of the red gore. Headless bodies lay in the scuppers and in one case a head rolled back and forth with the motion of the ship like an abandoned football. Everywhere it looked like the work of a butcher who had run amok with a cleaver, hacking and chopping in a frenzy of crazed bloodlust.

Still, badly hurt as she was, the *Warspite* carried on her duties, helping the dying garrison of the Greek island with what gunfire she could still muster. She eventually limped into Alexandria, trailing thick black smoke behind her, to unload her wounded, who were dying like flies now without skilled medical aid. Old ABC knew the ship needed all the aid he could give. Once the wounded had been ferried away, he hurried aboard, hoisted his own flag on her and ordered the ship's company to be assembled. He didn't waste words. He could see just how worn and disheartened the survivors were; far too many of them had lost their 'oppos', their long-term friends. They needed backbone and he was the man to give it to them.

Standing there on the bridge of the ruined ship, its steel decks gashed and lacerated by the scars of the bombings like the symptoms of some loathsome skin disease, he snapped, 'Don't go feeling sorry for yourselves . . . You're a hundred times better off than those poor brown jobs' – he meant the soldiers – 'trapped in Crete. They're stuck there. You can get away. So I say this to you, men: YOU MUST NOT THINK YOU'RE FINISHED OR ARE YET FINISHED WITH THE JOB ON HAND . . . YOU'VE GOT TO GO ON!'

It wasn't a great speech. It would never go down in the annals of classic oratory, but it had the effect that the old admiral wanted. The worn, hollow-eyed faces of the crew lit up. Their eyes glowed again with the enthusiasm of youth. Without any command from the captain or any of the senior officers, old CPO Higgins, the veteran of the Battle of Jutland, raised his battered, smoke-stained cap and yelled in a cracked voice, 'Three cheers for the C-in-C. Hip . . .'

It was a cry taken up by nearly a thousand throats. The danger, the damage, the deaths were abruptly forgotten. A hoarse shout rose into the afternoon sky, scattering the scavenging birds with fright. Up above them, that hard old man who commanded all their destinies and perhaps was now sending them back to their deaths, saw their excited young faces through a blurred mist. Slowly, two lone tears started to roll down his withered cheeks . . .

The Englishman was kind. There was no denying that. As best he could, in his pathetic bits and pieces of German and Italian, he explained to the amputees in the dusty prison compound how to get the best from the crude wooden artificial limbs which had been made for them by local Egyptian labour. Every now and again, he smiled encouragingly, willing each patient to get through the little obstacle course that the Medical Corps orderlies had erected, so that they could try out the limbs.

Whenever a patient fell or daren't try one of the obstacles on his own, he would volunteer his help, saying, '*Bene . . . bene . . .* very good, old chap'. Or '*Gut gut . . . das ist richtig, mein Freund.*' And despite the fact he was enemy and absurd with his overlong shorts, fat belly and outsized horn-rimmed glasses, the wounded officer prisoners warmed to him. That is all, except *Tenente* Breitmeyer, who sat in the sand, his new wooden left arm lying neglected at his side.

More than once, the fat English medical officer looked over at him as he slumped there apathetically, a sour smile on his face as he stared at the antics of the other amputees. The medical officer thought he might go across and have a few words with him, but always something distracted him, either one of the medical orderlies or their Italian POW assistants would be running over, calling to him to come and see one prisoner or another.

But as it grew progessively too hard to continue the exercises and the prisoners started to visibly fade, the fat MO called a halt to the proceedings, ordered a cool drink for his patients and, dabbing his plump, perspiring face, waddled over to where Breitmeyer slumped in the shade. It was customary to clamber to their feet and come to some semblance of attention when approached by an officer of the camp staff, but when Breitmeyer did not do so, the fat MO didn't seem offended. Indeed he cried, as if the POW was just about to carry out the military courtesy, 'Please don't get up, Lieutenant. It's far too hot just now.' Again he gave Breitmeyer the full benefit of that rosy, fat smile of his, eyes sparkling behind the horn rims.

Breitmeyer didn't react. He continued to look sour, one hand resting on the new artificial limb.

'Can't you get used to it?' he asked.

'I can,' Breitmeyer answered in newly improved English, 'but I will not.'

The MO's smile didn't change. 'You ought to,' he said slowly and carefully, as if he were afraid the prisoner might not understand him. 'You will need to when you are released to civvie street.' He saw that Breitmeyer didn't understand and added swiftly, 'When you become a civilian again. A man needs both arms.'

Breitmeyer sniffed. What fools these English are, he told himself contemptuously, encouraging me. If I had two hands, I'd strangle him straight off, the grinning fat baboon. Aloud he said, 'Need both arms – to do what?'

The MO said, 'I have just dealt with one of your chaps who stepped on a mine. His right leg was shredded to the thigh.' He touched his fat hip to indicate the extent of the wound. 'And the blast seared through his trousers, burning his penis and anus. You understand?'

Breitmeyer nodded, wondering what the fat fool was getting at.

'His testicles had to go, yet he feels he is a man. Though, of course, with women . . .' He didn't complete the rest of his sentence. Instead he said, 'Do you feel you are not a man because of your arm?'

Since they had amputated his arm after the torture in the *Warspite*, Breitmeyer had never encouraged anyone, friend or foe, to ask such a question. He wasn't going to allow it now, either. So he snapped, 'Sir, my arm is my personal affair. It is my problem. You English did it, you English will pay for it.' The venom in his voice and the sudden blaze of almost uncontrollable anger in his pale blue eyes made the fat MO start.

He seemed to jump backwards, saying, 'I only meant to help, Breitmeyer. That is all . . . Only help . . . Please, carry on.' Hastily he turned and strode away with short nervous steps, his fat buttocks wobbling as he did so; it was almost as if he couldn't get away quickly enough.

Breitmeyer grinned for the first time in many a week.

It wasn't a pleasant sight. Still, the one-armed prisoner did feel a small sense of triumph. He, a helpless, crippled prisoner of war, had actually frightened this fat smug self-satisfied English officer. It was a good feeling.

But that day, the crippled Italian of the once feared Black Devils would enjoy yet another triumph of a sort. Half an hour after the fat MO had dismissed the 'Crippled Legion', as Breitmeyer called his fellow amputees contemptuously, he was waiting outside the place's Dental Centre for Corporal Mario Stevens, or 'Eyetie Sheep's Arse', as he was known to his fellow RAMC technicians. Mario was very friendly. Under other circumstances, Breitmeyer might have thought the swarthy little Englishman with the Italian mother might have ulterior motives for the supply of litttle 'goodies' that he passed on. But in the camp, he felt that kind of relationship between a prisoner and member of the staff would have been nigh on impossible. Still Sheep's Arse might be useful, not only for the chocolate and cigarettes he provided, but also for the information which would be beyond value once he attempted to make his escape – and escape he would, cost what it may.

So, he lounged in the shade of the long wooden hut and ancilliary tents from which came the moans and groans of the soldiers from the surrounding camps, who came to receive their dental treatment here, wondering how long it would take before Sheep's Arse made his usual late-afternoon appearance at the back door, flashing him that tremendous blinding-white smile of his.

Idly he listened to the talk of the Tommies waiting for treatment, trying to understand their virtually incomprehensible slang which seemed to be a different language than the English he knew. 'Goes sick I does, cos the quack sez I should with me leg,' a tall skinny private with no teeth was telling his mate mournfully. 'And what did the silly bleeder at the Dental Centre do? Why, the frigger whips out all my choppers.'

His mate spat drily in the dust: 'They should have put the MI frigging bloke on a thick 'un. Jankers for the rest of his frigging days,' he said hotly. 'What a frigging Kate Karney.'

'Yer, but what can yer expect? Yer go sick with yer frigging leg and what does the army do? Why they pull out all yer frigging pearly gates. I tell yer, Gus, I'm bleeding browned off with going sick. Ain't no telling what they'll do to yer once them doctors get started.'

'You can say that agen, old mucker . . .'

Breitmeyer sighed. As far as he was concerned, the two soldiers could say it again a million times over and he still wouldn't understand what they were damn well talking about. He gave up and told himself that if the Eyetie Sheep's Arse didn't make his appearance soon, he could stick his cigarettes right up his own English arse.

But fortunately for Corporal Mario Stevens, he was fated not to make that particular attempt on his anus that afternoon. For five minutes later he was at the back door as usual, all gleaming teeth and shining pomaded hair, waving at the waiting Breitmeyer.

Cautiously Breitmeyer idled his way across; not that the soldiers waiting for treatment noticed. He was just another greasy wop. Sheep's Arse's big smile vanished when he saw the look on Breitmeyer's face and noted that he had his new artificial arm crooked at the elbow joint and hanging over his shoulder. 'Doesn't it fit correctly?' he asked and added swiftly, 'They take some time getting used to, you know.'

'I'm not wearing it,' Breitmeyer answered. 'Who wants to be a cripple?'

Sheep's Arse was going to console him, thought better of it and instead brought out a crumpled green cigarette packet from beneath his white overall. 'Here, these will cheer you up, old friend.' Five Woodbines.' He smiled. 'Worth their weight in gold these days in Alex . . . Got 'em off a bloke in the Fleet.' As he passed them over, he brushed his fingers against Breitmeyer's hand gently.

The latter pretended not to notice. It didn't matter anyway. He no longer smoked. These cigarettes would join the rest he was stockpiling for the day of his escape.

'Not that there'll be many more Woods for a while,' Sheep's Arse added. 'It's back to the camel dung soon, those bloody awful Victory fags.'

Breitmeyer thought he'd better show some interest, so he said, 'Why's that . . . er . . . Mario?' It was the first time he had used the corporal's first name, though the Englishman had asked him to do so several times.

Sheep's Arse blushed with pleasure. Without thinking he was giving away a military secret to an enemy alien as he answered in a whispered voice, 'Cos the fleet's doing a bunk. It's this Crete attack. They're clearing Alex. Even the old *Warspite*, in her state, is going too.'

'*Warspite*?' Breitmeyer pricked up his ears immediately at the mention of the hated name.

'Yer, when I saw her in Alex this morning, she was listing badly, all shot up and there was still black smoke coming from . . . er . . . the front bit, you know what I mean?'

Breitmeyer did. He beamed and said, 'I must go.'

Sheep's Arse looked disappointed. 'I thought we might talk a bit,' he sighed. 'It's char . . . er . . . tea up in five mins. I could get you a cup?'

Breitmeyer shook his head. He wanted to be alone with this new information. He couldn't waste time on the English 'warm brother' with his feminine sensitivities. 'Thank you for the cigarettes,' he said and turned, not giving the other man a chance to say any more. As he walked away to his tent, his mind racing electrically with the news about the damned *Warspite*, he heard the soldier called Gus say, '*Now* don't you tell 'em they took yer teeth out by mistake, or this time they might chop yer leg off . . . ha . . . ha!'

This time, a happy Breitmeyer half-felt he might even laugh at the comment . . .

On May 23, it was clear even to the most stupid matelot on the damaged *Warspite* that the naval intervention at Crete was about finished. That May day, the dogwatches, who had time to hang about and watch the action, saw the destroyer *Greyhound*, the cruisers *Fiji* and *Gloucester* and finally Lord Mountbatten's *Kelly* and her sister ship the *Kashmir*, fall victim to the German bombers which were everywhere.

Later that same day, it was announced from the bridge that the survivors of the island's allied garrison were soon to be evacuated. The Germans and their bomber fleets had proved too much for the Allies. The *Warspite* was to return to Alex, unload her wounded and then, patched up the best that could be done in a hurried emergency, she was to leave the Med for the time being, bound for some – as yet – unknown port.

Despite the defeat and the heavy casualties that the *Warspite* had suffered, the crew were overjoyed. 'Christ Almighty,' they said, 'there'll be white tarts agen . . . I might even recognize the old woman . . . First thing for me, mates, is a pint of good English wallop – maybe several! D'yer think they'll still be playing soccer? York City's top o' the Third Division now. Hell's bells, I'd pay as much as half a dollar to see the old team play agen . . .'

But amid the happiness and youthful enthusiasm of the *Warspite*'s matelots at the thought of returning to Britain and that old comfortable peacetime world of beer, women and soccer, there were a few who were assailed by more sombre thoughts as the old ship started to pull slowly away from Alexandria. Escorted by destroyers, circling the slow, damaged steel monster like anxious collies worried about a reluctant flock, the *Warspite* limped to sea, leaving behind an Africa disappearing quickly into the sudden darkness of nightfall.

Jim Hawkins found the old gunnery CPO Higgins leaning against the rail staring into the gloom. He had been drinking. Jim Hawkins could smell the heavy smell of neat rum even as he approached. But it didn't matter. Most of the crew had saved their tot till the evening to celebrate their departure from the Med for ports unknown. It was almost as if their war was over and they were moving into a brighter and better future.

Not for CPO Higgins. Hawkins felt his mood even before the old Chiefie responded to the traditional, 'Penny for 'em, Chiefie?'

It seemed to take the old petty officer a long time to react. Finally he said, still staring at the fading coastline, 'I was just thinking.'

'What, Chiefie?'

'That I won't see Alex no more. Perhaps none of us will.' Chiefie's thick rum-soaked voice was unusually subdued and reflective. 'The old *Warspite* is about knackered as it is – worn out, like somebody who gets old is knackered.' He coughed suddenly, thick and rasping, and Jim Hawkins was startled. Abruptly he realized just how old Chiefie was. And the *Warspite* was virtually as old, too.

'Cheer up, Chiefie,' he said with more enthusiasm than he felt. 'Never say die, Chiefie.'

The old petty officer didn't respond. He fell silent and the two of them, the old hand and the boy, stared at a vanishing Africa, each one of them wrapped in a cocoon of his own thoughts.

So, she limped away; the veteran of the Battles of Narvik and Matapan, the Malta convoys, the bombardments of the Western Desert, the disaster of Crete, vanishing into an uncertain future, while fifty miles away, a one-armed man in shabby khaki drill, pushed his way contemptuously through a robed, smelly mob of Arabs and Egyptians and disappeared into the noisy jungle of Alexandria's native quarter.

That same night, Old ABC sent out his last signal as commander of the *Warspite*. It expressed a hope and an enthusiasm that worn, old Admiral Cunningham did not really feel. Like the grand old battleship, he, too, was exhausted and at the end of his tether. Still, he knew the signal had to be dispatched.

It read: OPERATION WELL CARRIED OUT . . . THERE IS NO QUESTION THAT WHEN THE OLD LADY LIFTS HER SKIRTS, SHE CAN RUN!

BOOK THREE

Bari, Salerno
1943

There's a saying in the Navy that wherever there is fighting to be done, *Warspite* will surely be in it.

London Daily Mail, *June, 1943*

One

The red warning light glowed. In the cockpit of the lumbering Junkers 52, the co-pilot turned and mouthed the words 'Strap up!' Next to *Sturmbahnfuhrer* Breitmeyer, the Luftwaffe dispatcher nodded. Easily the grey-clad figure of the SS officer rose to his feet. Behind him the mixed bunch of Italians and Germans in the grey Luftwaffe coveralls did the same. They looked nervous in the bloody hue cast by the little warning light next to the door of the transport.

Fixing his own parachute strap, the dispatcher balanced his way to the door, grunted and opened it. The cold night air flooded in, whipping his coveralls about his skinny body. Behind Breitmeyer, one of the nervous Italians started to shiver and complain it was *molto frio*. Breitmeyer didn't notice. He was concentrating on the jump to come. He had jumped before behind enemy lines, but still he found it worrisome. With one arm he found it difficult to keep an important balance and later very hard to manage the shroud lines in any kind of a wind. Still, he had done it before safely and he'd do it again. If he didn't, he shrugged and used the formula adopted by his comrades of Skorzeny's SS Parachute Battalion 501 – a quick death and make a handsome corpse.

The red light changed to green. He forgot his doubts as if they had never even existed. He shuffled forward the final two paces. Behind him the motley crew of agents

73

and saboteurs did the same. He paused in the door, poised there as if he were on the top of a swimming pool's diving board, ready to make some spectacular showy dive into the pool below.

The dispatcher shouted 'GO!'

Next moment he went. He flung himself out of the antiquated three-engined transport into the darkness below, broken only by the faint flickering pink to his left which was the battleground. The wind struck him an almost physical blow across his face. He gasped. Helpless with his one arm, he was thrown around. The tailplane struck him a glancing blow. He yelled again. For an instant, bright red and silver stars exploded in front of his eyes and he blacked out.

When he came round, he was swinging gently to left and right, coming down in complete silence, the shroudlines above concealing the departing Junkers 52. Its job done, the old 'Auntie Ju' was heading back north to schnapps and pea soup and long sleep in Skorzeny's remote little base. For a moment, Breitmeyer wished fervently he was going with the Luftwaffe crew. Then he dismissed the thought as soft and self-seeking. He had a job to do – and this time it was against the hated English. He concentrated on his landing.

Now he was coming down more quickly. To his right he could just glimpse the blacked-out tumbledown shape of some poor peasant cottage. He fumbled awkwardly with his shroudlines. He didn't want to land there, even though the place might look like a ruin. Most Italian farmhouses did – the Italians were an improvident people. Still the peasants always had dogs, and he didn't want them to wake up the whole damn countryside to announce his arrival behind enemy lines.

Slowly, tugging hard with his one hand, sweating profusely with the effort, he drew away from the lone farm, heading for a hillside, dotted with the stunted outlines of what he guessed to be ancient olive trees.

Hastily he pulled up his knees and braced himself. But before he could cover his face a sudden gust of wind forced him into the trees, the branches whipping his face painfully. His nostrils were filled with the scent of resin. Next minute he was on the ground, panting hard, as if he had just run a great race. He had done it – arm missing or not.

For a moment or two he lay there, assessing his position, listening to the wind and the dying drone of the transport. There was no other sound. Where the others had landed, he didn't know or care. Each of them had his own separate task and objective. Let them get on with it. Now he had to get to the rendezvous on time; that was his priority. He glanced at the green-glowing dial of his wristwatch. He had plenty of time. But he wanted to make the rendezvous *before* the contact. During the last few months with Skorzeny's 'Hunting Commando', it was one of the rules he had made for himself and it had paid before.

He got to his feet. Hurriedly he folded the parachute as best he could and looked around for a place to bury it and his grey coverall. He wasn't prepared to dig a hole to do so. Anyway, if a peasant found the gear, he'd never report the find to the authorities. Silk was too precious. He'd keep the chute for himself and sell the silk on the black market. Breitmeyer, a man normally without a sense of humour, smiled at the thought of the silk bundled underneath his one arm one day being made into a pair of knickers to fit some ample Italian arse. Then he found a large hole in one of the olive trees and without hesitation stuffed the chute and the coveralls into it. Five minutes later, he was on his way to the rendezvous with the mysterious Carlo.

Despite his haste, the agent and guide was there before him. He smelt the man before he saw him; that typical odour of perfumed cigarette, cheap scent and garlic. It was unmistakeably Italian.

He dropped. Cautiously, keeping his head low and controlling his breath, Breitemeyer, pistol in hand, peered through the maize which lined the narrow country road. A pre-war little Fiat Bambino was parked in the shadows with a man leaning against it, outlined by the icy light of the stars, puffing solemnly at a cigarette. Instinctively Breitmeyer noted the bulge in his right-hand pocket which indicated that he was armed. Yet the Italian seemed strangely at ease, as if he weren't one bit worried that he was engaged in picking up an enemy agent: a highly dangerous course of action in Allied Occupied Italy these days.

Breitmeyer pursed his lips thoughtfully. Why? he asked himself, Why was this unknown contact lounging there in the middle of the night, smoking so carelessly – it was something that no man acute to the danger should do at this time of the night – and so very much at his ease? He didn't know the answer. All he knew was that the alarm bells, tuned by three years of war, now began to sound. Carefully, he freed the knife he kept in his sock and slipped it up his sleeve. Finally he straightened up and whistled softly. It was the signal.

The guide started. He turned, automatic in his hand. '*Wer da?*' he snapped in accented German.

'Otto.' Breitmeyer gave the password, the first name of his chief, Otto Skorzeny.

The man relaxed and came forward a few steps. But he didn't let go of his pistol. Instead, he lowered it to the side of his leg like a dentist does his pliers when he advances upon a nervous patient in order to pull a tooth. '*Kamerad,*' he said, again in German. It was the second part of the password.

Five minutes later they were crowded together in the tiny

car, the Italian driver's smell overpowering: that amalagm of garlic, scent and something else, which Breitmeyer could only describe to himself as contained fear. For the driver began boasting straightaway, babbling in Italian, that he had always been a loyal supporter of the Duce, a member of the *OVRA* no less and not ashamed to say so today when the Italian Gestapo, *Organizazione Vigilanza Repressione Antifascismo*, was hated throughout Italy and its members hunted down relentlessly.

Not that he was afraid of that, he continued, as he drove the little Fiat in his flashy arrogant manner, hurrying through silent villages, hand on horn, not giving a damn for what he might encounter in the mean, mud-heavy streets. Why, hadn't he been to America in the twenties and become a member of the Noble Society? He nudged Breitmeyer significantly. 'Even today the Mafia hold their hand over me. I am protected,' he boasted.

His boastfulness confirmed what Breitmeyer had suspected. He was one of those damned Sicilians who had joined the secret police on orders from their *Capi* when Mussolini had started to crack down on the Mafia in the late twenties. The man was a born survivor and survivors didn't risk their lives for lost causes like that of the Germans in Italy. The little ex-Mafioso would betray him at the drop of a hat. So what was the little runt, with his cunning dark eyes which wouldn't hold his gaze for longer than a second, up to?

Only half an hour later, when the Italian stopped the little car outside a road-worker's stone hovel just to the south of their turn-off at Altamura, did he come to some conclusion. The driver handed him a small bottle of grappa, saying, 'Hey, comrade, take a drink . . . it will warm you up. I have to speak a second with the old man. The organization, you know.' He smirked in the faint, ugly white light of the dawn and turned to the unshaven old man, who mended the road and who had just emerged from his fetid-smelling hovel, rubbing the sleep out of his eyes.

What the organization was, Breitmeyer couldn't guess. Perhaps it was just a pretext to stop here. But whatever it was, he didn't like this unscheduled stop. Still, he said nothing. Obediently he took a slug of the fiery spirit and felt it surging pleasantly through his chilled, stiff body, all the while straining his ears to see if he could catch anything of their whispered conversation. But it was conducted in some local dialect, which Breitmeyer couldn't understand, though by the meaningful glances the old road-worker cast in his direction, he guessed that the two of them were talking about him. But what?

Half an hour later they were on their way again, circling the city and heading south towards the port of Bari: his target.

Now as it grew lighter, the little car had to, more than once, drive swiftly off the road to avoid being run down by the great convoys of Allied vehicles, tanks, trucks, troop transports, leaving the supply port. And on both sides there were piles of petrol cans, ammunition boxes and the like indicating, as Skorzeny had suspected, that the English were probably soon going to launch an offensive on this coast to coincide with the landing they had just made beneath Naples at the beach of Salerno.

Now the runtish driver started to get inquisitive. More than once he nodded at the great piles of supplies, guarded by mostly black soldiers with fixed bayonets, stating point-edly, 'Do you think the English will now attack soon?'

Breitmeyer refused to be drawn. All the same, he was assailed by nagging doubts about the Italian wanting infor-mation from him before they hit Bari. But why? What was the Italian going to do when they reached the port? His job was simply to deliver him to the outskirts and then he, Breitmeyer, would make his own way to his next rendezvous. This was standard operational procedure in the Hunting Commando. Each of the agents behind the Allied lines was supposed to know only a little piece of the overall plan. It was safer that way. Slowly, he started to realize he had to make a decision. It was brutal in its simplicity: did he kill the Italian or did he let him live and chance what might result from that decision . . . ?

When Gottraut Breitmeyer had come home from Russian captivity in 1919, he was a fervent anti-Bolshevik, and to his surprise, suddenly stateless. He had departed in 1914 as a sergeant in an Imperial and Royal Austrian mountain regiment, and returned a lieutenant to find that his part of the Austrian Empire was currently being disposed of at Versailles by the victors, Britain, America and Italy.

Returning to his high Alpine farm above Bozen, which had suddenly been transformed into Bolzano, he had waited till a decision had been made. After all, he was the *Erbbauer*, the hereditary farmer, as the senior son was always called and, as was the custom in those remote Alpine valleys and high meadows, it was the duty of the eldest son to ensure that the family farm survived, come what may. By 1920, Gottraut Breitmeyer had been transformed into an Italian citizen, just like so many of his one-time Austrian fellow citizens who had become Hungarians, Czechs, Slovenes, even Minor Russians. But, unlike so many of his fellow South Tyroleans, he had not left his homeland and transferred to what was left of a defeated Austria. He had stayed on at his remote farm; indeed he had married one of the new Italian immigrants from the south that the new Italian dictator, Mussolini, was pumping into the freshly gained South Tyrol to turn it into an Italian province. Young Breitmeyer had been the first product of this mixed marriage, growing up in those high meadows, remote from the affairs of the new Italy in the valleys below, speaking both the native German dialect and his mother's Italian.

When, in the new spirit of German nationalism, encouraged by the Nazi Party under a certain Herr Hitler, a fellow Austrian who lived in exile in Bavaria, his schoolmates blew up Italian power stations and attacked remote Italian *carabinieri* posts, Breitmeyer continued peacefully with his studies, which he hoped would take him out of the rough-and-tumble of mountain farming and perhaps to the University of Rome. Even when it seemed that Hitler, now the new German Chancellor and soon to be head of an incorporated Austrian Republic too, would demand the return of the South Tyrol from his fellow dictator Mussolini, Breitmeyer did not concern himself with the politics of the matter. He was content to continue on the path he had planned for himself.

But at the age of eighteen, after he had successfully finished high school in Bolzano, he discovered the University of Rome was out. Mussolini didn't want too many educated South Tyroleans who might well form the nucleus of a South Tyrolean independence movement in the fashion of young intellectuals. Still, the ban had not changed his attitude. He had opted for the Italian navy which was expanding rapidly, volunteering for the technical wing so that he might obtain a higher qualification in that manner.

It had been a wrong move. The traditionalists of the Royal Italian Navy, who had fought against the Austrians and Germans in World War One, had not accepted a young hopeful, who looked German, spoke German and came from that newly acquired Italian province that was becoming more problematic than Sicily and the Mafia. Slowly but surely young Breitmeyer had come to realize that he seemed to belong nowhere. He was neither German nor Italian. He was, it appeared, fated to become an outsider.

For a while his membership of the Black Devils, filled with bright, intelligent, daredevil young men who were perhaps patriots but were really adventurers, had made him forget that feeling of being an outsider. That had, however, been long ago. Much water had flowed under the bridge. Since then some of the surviving Black Devils had gone over to the Anglo-Americans, Italy's new allies, some had gravitated to the Germans, who occupied the north of their country, with the deposed Mussolini now acting as German lackey. But the old spirit had probably gone.

It was for that reason he had volunteered to serve under another adventurer and an Austrian to boot, Skorzeny, who led Germany's Hunting Commando, those daredevils of half a dozen nationalities who fought that cruel war in the shadows, behind the enemy lines where no quarter was given or expected. It was the kind of life that Breitmeyer had taken to immediately, just as he had once done the same with the Black Devil Squadron. It was the kind of fighting formation in which patriotism and nationality didn't count – just guts.

The gigantic Austrian commando leader, whose scarred face looked like the work of a crazy horse-butcher armed with a cleaver, had been fascinated by Breitmeyer's tale of how he had been the only Axis prisoner to escape from Africa back to Italy. He had taken him on immediately, embracing him in his apelike grasp in the effusive Austrian fashion. Thereafter he had given Breitmeyer numerous dangerous missions in Italy, where his perfect, fluent knowledge of the language had been particularly useful now that Italy had signed a separate peace with the Western Allies and Germany was starved of knowledge of what was going on in the southern tip of the country.

It had been the kind of task that Breitmeyer had enjoyed. He had become a lone wolf with virtually every man's hand against him, fighting not only the Allies, but also the Italian intelligence services working for them and the all-powerful Italian communist partisan movement which took its orders from Moscow and which worked not only against the Germans, but the Allied 'capitalists' and their right-wing Italian royalist supporters. Now, Breitmeyer reasoned, as the little car rolled ever closer to Bari and Allied military traffic grew thicker and thicker, he was facing perhaps a new enemy – the hidden might of the Mafia in the form of the little runt at the wheel, and he was under no illusions about the Mafiosi. Those crooks would betray even their own grandmothers for a handful of *lire*.

Thirty minutes later, his decision was made for him just as they were approaching the outskirts of Gruma, a small place some twenty kilometres to the west of Bari. By now, the runt had lapsed into a gloomy, brooding silence, obviously resigned to the fact he was not going to get any more out of his passenger about his contacts in the port. The silence had pleased and yet discomforted Breitmeyer. It gave him time to think about his next move once the driver had dropped him off on the outskirts of Bari. At the same time he was worried about the brooding look on the driver's sallow, pockmarked face. He knew these sour-faced Sicilian looks of old; they did not bode well. The driver was up to no good. The question was what did he intend?

As they slowed down again, Breitmeyer took a firmer grip of his hunting knife just in case and stared cautiously to both left and right. Here the main highway was lined with the usual tumbledown Italian houses, interspersed with *tavernas* and bars, which to judge from their signs 'Texas' 'New York' and the like, were used by the US truck drivers who plied the route from Bari to Italy's western coast where the new attack by the US 5th Army was taking place.

But it wasn't the helmeted black American drivers who

caught the commando's attention as they wandered in and out of the bars, sometimes accompanied by slatternly women who were plying their trade in the back of the American trucks even this early. It was the small group of erect figures wearing red caps, their shoulder straps painted a brilliant white, boots highly polished despite the mud, standing watchfully at the next crossroads.

'Redcaps!' he hissed under his breath. For he remembered the type from Alexandria and his flight to Cairo. They were the tough, hard-boiled British military policemen, recognizable by their red caps, feared by both soldiers and civilians alike. For nothing seemed to escape their eagle eye.

'What did you say?' the driver asked, not taking his shifty gaze from the crossroads.

Breitmeyer was about to explain. Then thought better of it. The driver had seen the military policemen all right and, unlike the reaction of most Italians at the sight of a policeman, he didn't seem one bit worried. Indeed, a cunning little smile was beginning to form on his thin cruel lips beneath the pencil-slim moustache, which looked as if he might paint it on every morning after he'd shaved.

With a shock of instant recognition, Breitmeyer realized that the Italian driver had been looking for these enemy policemen for the last half an hour. He was expecting them and by the way the group of redcaps had turned and were staring at the little car, slowly weaving its way in and out of the military traffic, *they* were expecting him. He was riding straight into the trap he had been anticipating all along.

Slowly the driver started to change down.

Breitmeyer reacted. His nerves started to tingle excitedly. He felt the rush of adrenaline. His breath suddenly was coming in short, sharp, barely controlled gasps. Abruptly he realized he was sweating profusely. He gripped the keen blade more tightly, his hand wet with perspiration. 'Why . . . why are you slowing down?' he asked.

The driver didn't seem to hear. He changed again into second. Over at the MP post, the tallest of the redcaps had started unslinging his Sten gun purposefully. Now Breitmeyer knew that they were waiting for him.

'Keep moving!' he commanded sharply.

The driver didn't take his eyes off his front. Out of the side of his mean rat-trap mouth he sneered, 'You have nothing more to say.'

'That's what you think,' Breitmeyer snapped. He was ready to move. 'Now do as I say.'

The driver wasn't listening.

Breitmeyer acted. In one and the same action, he pressed the blade close to the surprised driver's ribcage and slammed his foot down on the former's holding the accelerator. The car shot forward. The driver cried, '*Porco di Madonna* . . . Are you crazy!' Narrowly he missed a jeep and, swerving right, tried desperately to get his foot free.

To no avail! Breitmeyer kept his down hard. 'Just keep driving!' he yelled above the shouts and curses from the US jeep which had careened off into the drainage ditch on the left.

Now the redcaps reacted. They ran into the road. The tallest started to unsling his Sten. He spread his legs in the fashion of a gunslinger and Breitmeyer knew instinctively what he would do. He'd stand his ground, once the little Fiat was in range, he'd loose off a volley from the machine pistol, shattering the windscreen and blinding the Italian driver. '*Denkste!*' Breitmeyer roared furiously in German.

Still keeping his foot down hard on top of the Italian's, he pressed the sharp point of his dagger harder into the Italian's ribs. 'Now listen,' he yelled above the racket of the engine. 'When I say right, through that hedge and—'

The sharp burr of the Sten drowned the rest of his

words. Slugs howled off the chassis. The far corner of the windscreen shattered into a gleaming spider's web of broken glass. The Italian's face suddenly looked as if someone had thrown a handful of strawberry jam at it. He screamed and let go of the wheel. The car raced forward out of control. Breitmeyer saw the look of utter horror on the redcap's face as he realized it wasn't going to stop. He threw up his hands. The Sten dropped. It seemed as if he were attempting to protect his face. Too late! The car went into him with an unholy thud of metal striking human flesh. He disappeared from sight and then the car was rocketing off the road into the field to the right, still keeping going despite the dead or dying Italian slumped moaning over the shattered controls.

Moments later the fugitive SS man was running for his life, zig-zagging crazily through the shoulder-height maize, the pistol bullets slicing the heavy cobs off to left and right of him, with the wrecked car burning furiously behind him . . .

Two

'How many times have I told you, Corporal,' Captain Jo-Ann Kaplan said with mock weariness, 'that when the casualties come in, they've got to have their weapons removed and their ID at the ready. How can we keep up with regs, if you don't observe procedures?' She sighed as if her fat shoulders were carrying the cares of the world.

Outside, the medics and their Italian assistants were processing a new bunch of US Army casualties, getting them ready for the doctors who would soon pass through the lines of stretchers, making their assessments of the men's wounds and how they should be treated. Wounded men were crying out for water, drugs, and in some cases in shame-faced voices for some place to 'take a crap, before I fill my goddam pants!' Not that the big-nosed, pasty-faced nursing sister heard the cries; she had long ago been hardened to the plight of the wounded.

'Yes, Captain, ma'am,' the young bespectacled sergeant said dutifully. 'I'll see to it.'

In her usual domineering manner, the ugly female officer wasn't satisfied. She never was, especially when it was one of the hospital's male staff who had transgressed against some order or other. 'It's no use saying you'll see to it, Dombrowski,' she barked. 'You always say that. See to it *now*!' Her pasty face suddenly flushed with anger. 'Goddamit, how many times have I to tell you men. All you have in your goddam heads is babes and booze—' The rest of her words were drowned by the shrill alarm signal ringing up and down the corridors of the US military hospital, indicating that another batch of ambulances was bringing yet more casualties which had been shipped around the boot of Italy from the beach at Salerno and deposited here for treatment. 'Kay,' she raised her voice shrilly, sounding like some frustrated spinster schoolmarm, Dombroski couldn't help thinking, 'off you go and don't forget those damned dogtags.'

'Yes, ma'am,' the young soldier said, happy to escape. He grabbed his garrison cap and notebook and was gone before she had the chance to make any further complaints while she stared severely at his departing back, telling herself, as she did often, that without her the 54 US Field Hospital would fall apart.

For a moment or two she stared out at the stretchers being laid out in the courtyard of the former *palazzo* below. Beyond them, a crowd of shabby Italians were peering through the railings, some of them actually holding out their hands for cigarettes and those damned caramels of theirs, begging from the wounded. What a people, she told herself, trying to panhandle wounded GIs. They deserved everything they got. The next time she conferred with the MP lieutenant in charge of hospital security, she'd make a point of seeing that such crowds of onlookers would be cleared when wounded were being off-loaded.

Then suddenly, quite startlingly, she smiled, revealing her ugly mouth filled with yellow teeth, big and square like chiselled gravestones. For she had just remembered she had promised Stella she would see her at three that afternoon. And the Italian orderly, with those warm, liquid dark eyes of hers always cheered her up, took her mind off this brutal male world in which men got killed, and when they were not killing each other, were solely concerned with getting drunk and, as they put it in their customary crude masculine manner, 'getting inside dames' pants!'

She looked at her reflection in the glass of the hospital corridor and pulled a face. Men, how she just hated them!

Outside now, the wounded were being moved as if on a factory conveyor belt. They were unloaded from the meat wagons which had brought them from the landing craft and the hospital ship anchored further out in the bay, and deposited in silent or moaning rows on the ground, their clothes blood- and mud-stained, the stretchers, here and there, dripping blood. Immediately the medics, the Italian orderlies and doctors went to work, sorting them, pulling off bandages to yells of pain and protest, digging fingers into suppurating wounds, sniffing damaged feet and hands for the first tell-tale signs of gas gangrene, peering at the morphine dosages pencilled on the wounded men's foreheads, here and there whipping their scalpels across the windpipes of those who were choking for air or beating madly on chests when patients seemed to be going under.

She nodded her satisfaction and was pleased with how the men were tackling this new batch of wounded. There'd be more before the day was out, but the morning intake was always the worst. After all, they had brought them in overnight in an attempt to hide the extent of the US casualties from the Italian civilians and, in some cases, the wounded hidden in the ships' holds had been waiting for hours for real medical attention.

She dismissed the scene and stared out at the latest arrivals at Bari, filling the crowded supply port even more. They were limeys, she had been told from a great cumbersome battleship of World War One vintage which had bombarded the whole of the Italian coastland from Reggio to Brindisi in support of the limey advance up the boot of Italy. Now, she guessed, they were soon on their way to the east Italian coast to support the US 5th Army landing at Salerno. She sniffed. She'd better warn Stella. These limey sailors were just as bad as American gobs; their only thought when they were granted shore leave was to get stinking and lay the first available female. Yes, Stella had to be warned. The goddam fleet was back in town . . .

Petty Officer Jim Hawkins looked at his liberty men. They were all very young and HO men – 'Hostilities Only'. But then these days, he told himself, they all were. The old regular navy had virtually been wiped out over the three years of war. Now, even petty officers were like himself, twenty-one-year-olds who had been promoted rapidly as the casualties had mounted. Undoubtedly, poor old Higgins, who had disappeared on the Russian convoy, would have been in his thirties before he had achieved the rank of petty officer.

Still, despite his youth, Hawkins knew his business – and his young sailors. 'All right then,' he snapped as his gun crew tugged at their jerseys and adjusted their white caps for the umpteenth time, 'I want you bunch of fairy queens to note this.'

Someone said in a simpering falsetto, 'Kiss me quick, Petty Officer. Me mother's drunk.'

Hawkins ignored the remark. The lads were in high spirits. Let them have their day of fun. They didn't get many of them these days, and once they were off Salerno they were in for a lot of hard graft and possibly grief. The Jerries were giving the navy some stick there.

'Keep yer noses clean. If you want yer grog, drink in moderation. If you want the other!'

The young sailors smirked at the mention of 'other'; they all knew what the smart keen petty officer meant. For his part, Hawkins told himself that probably most of them were still virgins, but then sailors always had to boast that they were God's gift to womanhood and that they had a judy in every port.

'Remember to carry out the proper drill. Wear a French letter and afterwards straight off to the nearest pro station to get that nasty thing you have between yer legs cleaned up by the sick-bay attendants. If you don't and you catch a dose,' he added his warning, 'you'll be on a fizzer, right on the rattle *toot sweet* and facing the old man for self-inflicted wounds.' He relaxed and smiled at them. 'All right, enjoy yersens and don't forget – *don't miss the liberty boat, or else* . . . Dismiss.'

The excited young sailors needed no urging. They were off immediately, heading for the side to be scrutinized by the officer of the watch as they saluted and went down the ladder to the steam pinnace waiting to take them into Bari.

Hawkins forced a slightly weary smile as he watched them go, chatting and shouting excitedly. Like all young matelots, they were full of piss and vinegar. He'd probably been like that himself back in 1939. But the war soon tamed them before it killed them. Let them enjoy their time out of battle. It would be all too short.

He dismissed his crew and concentrated on the great fleet of merchantmen and warships assembling in the southern Italian port. It was clear why. The Yanks were taking a beating at Salerno. Now they had two alternatives. Either they withdrew from their precarious beachhead and tried somewhere else further up the coast, or they slugged it out. In the latter case they'd need supplies, reinforcements and above all, the firepower of ships like the good old *Warspite*.

He sighed suddenly. As old as she was, there seemed no respite for the *Warspite*. Ever since her lengthy refit in the States and return to the Med, almost two years after she had limped away from the inland sea, she had been in constant action. Now she was wearing out again. He and the few remaining old hands on board could see that all too clearly. The engines weren't delivering full power, her ammunition supply apparatus went on the blink all the time and the gun barrels of her massive 15-inch guns were beginning to wear out again. As Able Seaman Hairless Harry, one of the few of the 1941 crew to be still on board two years later, was wont to comment in his thick Barnsley accent: 'She's like an old nag who ought to be sent out to pasture, but'll end in the knackers' yard ready to be turned into glue.'

Hawkins' handsome, yet emaciated face grinned a little at the thought. Hairless Harry was right, but he'd never admit it to a living soul. HMS *Warspite* would never be put out to pasture. She'd fight to the bitter end, going down with her drums beating and her colours flying.

It was then that he spotted the US merchantman, which was soon going to cause all the trouble and indirectly bring about the end of the *Warspite*, though not in the manner that Petty Officer Hawkins foresaw. It was plodding slowly into the anchorage, all alone, untended even by a tug. He tugged at the end of his sunburnt nose. There was something strange about the American ship, he felt even then at first sight. Normally merchantmen, usually coming from Oran or one of the other African ports, were accompanied by fellow merchantmen in a kind of makeshift convoy, even by destroyers when they were carrying troops or other important cargo for the front. Why had this one risked German subs and aircraft to make the long slow journey to Italy by herself? Strange. He lifted his glasses and focused them on the ship nudging its way through the water-borne traffic. He ran the glasses along her rigging. No bunting. Not even the usual stuff indicating that she was entering harbour. There was no clue to what she was carrying, and she could be carrying anything from highly dangerous shells to the soldiers' delight – spam.

Petty Officer Hawkins' frown deepened. Very strange. He lowered the binoculars a little and focused on the ship's name and the name of her home port. She was a Yankee all right, as he had guessed from her lines. Her home port was New York. Then he looked at the strange ship's name: USS *John Harvey*. He sniffed. The name meant nothing to him. But as he lowered his glasses and the *John Harvey* moved at a snail's pace towards Pier 26, Petty Officer Jim Hawkins little realized that the name would be burned on to his mind till the day he died . . .

High above Bari, someone else watched the entrance of the strange American ship that day. Not that he had any particular interest in it, as such. It was just part of the great mass of enemy ships which he was observing and counting in preparation for what was soon to come. Indeed, this was the reason he had undergone so many tribulations and dangers to reach Bari. And tired as he was, *Sturmbahnfuhrer* Breitmeyer felt his spirits uplifted as he realized that he had not been sent on one of the wild goosechases that he had experienced before ever since Skorzeny had recruited him for his Hunting Commando.

His eyes glittered with excitement and renewed energy as his gaze swept the great anchorage, packed with merchantmen, landing barges, lighters and troop transports, all busy with loading and unloading cargo, supplies and troops. Luftwaffe HQ in Rome had been right. This was going to be the main Allied supply port for the attack on Rome out of the Salerno beaches. Knock out Bari and its shipping and the Allied offensive up the coast towards the Italian capital might be stalled till the spring and by then the situation might well have changed in the German favour.

Suddenly Breitmeyer gasped with surprise. Immediately, he ceased his scrutiny of the supply port and turned his attention to the outer anchorage and the ships stationed out there. Yes, there was no mistaking that silhouette. Why, the outline had been etched on his mind's eye ever since that terrible day in 1941 when the Tommies had chained him to the ship's hull and left him until his wounded arm had to be amputated to save him from dying with gangrene. It was the *Warspite*.

He sat back on his heels, suddenly panting hard, as if he were running some kind of a race, his mind whirling. Out of the blue that image and time had re-appeared, infiltrating into his consciousness like some terrible nightmare come back to haunt him. He licked his abruptly parched lips, knowing that he ought not to linger here on the bluff much longer. Some enemy patrol might come across him and begin asking awkward questions. Still, he was as if transfixed, seemingly unable to rise and slink away for his rendezvous with his contact.

It was the *Warspite*. Over the years, it had been the ship and not the people who had manned her back in Alexandria, which had become the object of his burning hatred. Their faces had vanished into time, becoming just blurred images which today he probably couldn't even identify. But not the ship in which it had all happened. He would never forget HMS 'damned' *Warspite*! Now, as he squatted there on his heels, he wondered excitedly how he might exact his revenge. The plan had not included attacks on naval vessels. It had been the supply ships and the troop transports that the Luftwaffe High Command had wanted knocking out. They were the ships that would make the Salerno surprise landings succeed if they were not knocked out in time. In this case, the enemy capital ships were not so important. All the same, this was a golden opportunity. Could he convince Luftwaffe command to change their plans at this late stage of the game?

He stopped. His ears had taken in the well-remembered plod of infantry – the poor bloody infantry – the clink of entrenching tools, the grunts of men weighed down with equipment like pack animals. Instantly, he was on the alert. There was some kind of infantry patrol panting their way up the steep hillside. If they found him here, even in civilian clothes, surveying the harbour and shipping below with field glasses, Zeiss of Germany to boot, they'd be damned stupid if they didn't begin asking awkward questions.

Swiftly, he pulled back in a slither of stones and earth till he reached a grove of trees, inside which there was a thick clump of bushes. Ignoring the thorns that ripped at his shabby civilian suit, he wriggled in backwards and lay still. The patrol came closer. Instinctively he knew they wouldn't spot him. Why should they? They weren't looking for him. Besides he knew, too, that he had been selected, somehow or other, to carry out a vital task before he died. It was to sink that symbol of English cruelty – HMS *Warspite* . . .

She couldn't contain herself. Indeed, her hands were tingling in suppressed excitement and were trembling as if she had been on the booze for days on end. Although it was only ten minutes till the time when she was scheduled to meet Stella, she walked briskly down the hall to the officers' latrines, selecting the furthest which was reserved for women officers and, looking as if she was just goofing off for a break and a cigarette, stepped inside.

She stopped, and with a hand that trembled badly, ripped down her olive, drab, issue knickers. She was soaking wet already at just the mere thought. She parted her legs. She felt sick with excitement, passion and wild lust. A man had never excited her like this. Indeed, they had always sickened her afterwards. It had taken all her effort not to vomit after she had cleaned herself once they had finished all that panting, heaving and thrusting and fallen across her body, lathered with sweat and exhausted.

This was different. Delicate, slow, thrilling. Tentatively she drew one wetted finger between her legs. She shivered. It took her all her strength not to cry out loud with the sheer naked passion of it. Before her mind's eye she conjured up the image of her body: naked, small-breasted, vulnerable and yet at the same time tremendously attractive; seductive with the faint patch of black down at the base of her stomach like that of some innocent virginal schoolgirl.

But she wasn't virginal . . . nor innocent, was she? By God she wasn't! She stroked herself again, parting the damp bush of hair, fighting not to give way to temptation and carry on wildly, furiously until her body exploded with relief from this almost unbearable passion.

She remembered the other times with her. That cunning little middle finger . . . the tip of the pink tongue . . . Oh no, she must not think of that . . . that tongue that *ton* . . . *gue* . . . Desperately, frantically, she bit back the scream of pure ecstasy as her loins were flooded with that rush of unbearable passion and lust. She sagged, sobbing for breath, as if she were badly hurt, her head sunk, her face glazed with hot sweat.

Her heart was beating madly, as if it might burst out of her ribcage at any moment. Numbly, her blank gaze took in the crude cartoon pencilled on the bottom of the lavatory door. It showed the rear end of an enormous elephant with a tiny mouse gazing up at the massively endowed creature and saying in awe: 'How true. The higher the formation the bigger the balls!'

It meant nothing to her. In her crazed, confused state it did not register, but the sudden dire wail over the port of the air-raid sirens did. A raid was on the way. Wearily, her limbs feeling like lead, she started to pull up her damp drawers.

Breitmeyer looked up at the bright afternoon sky as soon as

the sirens commenced wailing. It was an automatic gesture that all frontline troops indulged in. They had to. Death came from the skies, however blue and sunny.

High over the blinding glare of the sea out in the anchorage, there was a black dot poised in the sky, seeming almost motionless. He narrowed his eyes against the sun. Yes, he could just make it out. It was a four-engined German Focker Wulf reconnaissance plane – the Kondor, as they were called by German propaganda. There were only a few hundred of them in service. Normally they would be too precious to waste on a land-based recce op. Not now, however. The Luftwaffe was planning a major strike. Even Kondors would be authorized for an attack of that magnitude.

Now the ships of the fleet out in the further reaches of the anchorage had taken up the challenge. Even the *Warspite* had joined in the hasty barrage. Everywhere the sky to the east was peppered by angry black balls of flak. The pilots of the great four-engined plane didn't seem to notice. Majestically they sailed above the flak, taking their photographs and estimating the positions of the Allied fleet assembled below: a perfect, stationary target.

Breitmeyer nodded his approval. But then, as more and more guns began to join in and frightened Italian civilians further down the street started to run for cover, he realized that this was the ideal time to make contact. He forgot the Kondor and the great surprise soon to come, and set off.

Breitmeyer was not the only one alerted by the appearance of that lone four-engined German reconnaissance plane over Bari and the great fleet of merchantmen and warships assembling in its anchorage. Petty Officer Hawkins had been alerted and then alarmed by it. Although he was only a low-ranking petty officer of no great importance in the hierarchy of the great old battlewagon which reached up to a full admiral, he felt his duty was to register his alarm to his superior. Instead of following his gun crew to the sordid pleasures of Bari's waterfront, he reported to 'Guns', the senior officer in charge of the ship's artillery.

Guns, otherwise known as Lt. Commander Waterhouse, much younger than the World War One veteran who had occupied that post at the beginning of the war when Hawkins had first joined the ship, was receptive. He sat Hawkins down and said, after a red-faced and awkward Hawkins had explained his reason for his request 'through channels' to see him, 'You did right, Hawkins. It's good to see that you younger petty officers are so concerned about the welfare of the old lady.' – He meant the *Warspite* – 'As soon as I spotted the Hun, I asked myself what the bugger was up to. But, excuse me, have a gasper.' He pushed the silver cigarette box across his table towards Hawkins.

Hesitantly the younger man took one and fiddled with it, wondering how he should light it when Waterhouse indicated the heavy silver lighter. 'Between you and me,' Waterhouse went on, 'the *Warspite* is beginning to wear out again after the Yankee refit. Our ack-ack guns wouldn't be up to facing a major and prolonged air attack. But I don't have to tell you that. You people in 'A' turret know that we're a bit of an old crock.' He smiled winningly at the embarrassed petty officer who was finding it difficult to light the cigarette; as usual, anything left out in the air on board the battleship for any length of time became damp.

'Yessir. I know.'

'So, with the captain's permission, I took the liberty of phoning the Brylcreem chaps at their HQ' – he meant the RAF – 'and asking them what they thought. Could we expect a major Hun air raid during the period we're here in port? They bullshitted a bit if you'll forgive my French. But in the end, they put me through to RAF Intelligence – if there is such a thing?' He chuckled maliciously and Hawkins gave a weak, uncertain smile. 'And they swore on a stack of Bibles that the Huns didn't have the capacity. They'd be lucky, according to them, if they could field a dozen crates for an attack . . .'

And that had been that. Hawkins had gone away, accepting the gunnery officer's explanation that the Kondor had merely been on a recce mission to spot what kind of fleet the Allies were assembling in Bari for the attack on Salerno. There'd be no aerial follow-up. And with that he had to be satisfied . . .

A mile away, waiting for the American nurse and knowing that the end of the affair was, thank God, in sight, Stella Ricci had felt a sense of relief at the sight of the lone German plane. She knew that there was danger ahead, not only for the citizens of Bari and their Anglo-American occupiers, but also for herself. In two hours she'd meet her SS contact and pass on all the information she had collected at such cost. Then she would be in real danger. One wrong move and the enemy would put her in front of a firing squad; she had no illusions about that. But once that was over, she'd flee. Bari would see her no more. The whole nauseating, disgusting, animal business would be over.

But there would be no real escape for any of them. Within the next forty-eight hours, all of them without exception would be swamped by the terrible tragedy to come . . .

Three

'Smiling Albert', his soldiers called him. For the Field
Marshal always seemed to be displaying his tomblike
yellow front teeth in what they took to be a smile and in
the German army it was rare that high-ranking officers
smiled at the ordinary, common-or-garden infantrymen –
'the stubble-hoppers'.

But today, as he squatted in the sandbagged forward
observation post high above the Salerno beachhead, surrounded by his elegant glittering staff officers, Field Marshal Albert Kesselring was not smiling for once. There was
nothing to smile about for those who viewed the bloody
slaughter taking place half a kilometre below.

The Field Marshal swept his high-powered binoculars
from the sea, with its shattered barges and half-submerged
bodies of those who had fallen in the initial assault and had
still not been picked up. He mused that they seemed like
a khaki-coloured carpet laid from the water right up on to
the sandy beach. He focused on a little Italian girl, with
what looked like her stomach blown out, in the wreckage
of a house with beds hanging out like shreds in the holed
stone walls. Next to her an *Ami* leaned on his upturned
rifle, shoulders shaking uncontrollably, crying bitterly as
if he were heartbroken. All around him slugs whined off
the walls of the house and tracer zipped in a lethal morse
only metres away. He didn't seem to notice.

Kesselring gave a little sigh. Professional soldier he

101

might be, but he still, he told himself, possessed a heart. He could understand the enemy soldier's horror. All the same, he was a damn fool. If he didn't get under cover soon, he'd be as dead as the girl.

He swung his glasses away to the beach. Despite the horrendous casualties the Anglo-Americans had incurred in the initial landing, they were still pushing in more troops, cost what it may. And his artillery and air cover were waiting for them. Now, as the broad white V of the assault craft indicated they were now coming in at speed, the slaughter commenced once more. Over the artillery positions dug in the surrounding hills the green signal flares hissed into the ugly grey sky. It was the command 'Open fire!' Instinctively, Kesselring, the old soldier, open his mouth against the blast to prevent his eardrums from being burst. As he did so, the German fighter bombers came zooming in at ground level, cannon chattering, angry scarlet cannon shells hissing towards the barges like a swarm of disturbed hornets. Immediately all hell broke loose.

An immense barrage of flak arose immediately from the fleet. The Messerschmitts seemed to be flying through an interlinking network of flying steel, bright cherry-red explosions and clouds of thick grey smoke. Here and there planes staggered visibly. It was as if they had suddenly run into solid stone walls. Next moment they were screaming down to the sea, streaming black smoke behind them, their wings dropping off like great metal leaves, pilots screaming in silent hysteria as they battled to open their cockpits – in vain.

Still the others pressed home their attack, as on the heights the German 88s thundered, tearing the air apart with the sound of a great piece of canvas being ripped as their shells plummeted down on the frail little boats, lifting them out of the water and smashing them to matchwood like children's toys, tossing the bodies in a dozen different directions.

Yet despite those terrible attacks, Kesselring knew that the second or third wave of the assault troops would make the beach. They were equally determined. And soon, he guessed, when the enemy heavy ships appeared – he'd already heard of the presence of the British battleships in the Eastern Mediterranean – the attackers would have the artillery firepower to take on his 88s. With a little sigh, he lowered his glasses and left the attack to go as it would.

Immediately the orderlies started to pass out the tiny metal glasses filled with *grappa* and unpacked the staff's sandwiches. For although Smiling Albert was greatly admired by his common soldiers – those famed stubble-hoppers of his – he did demand all the privileges of his rank. His ample figure bore testimony to that.

The Field Marshal swallowed a slice of *blutwurst* by itself, disdaining the bread, washing it down with a shot of the fiery *grappa*, and announced quite simply, 'Four days, *meine Herren*. We move back in exactly four days from now. I have made my decision.'

'Need that be, *Herr Generalfeldmarschall*?' one of his staff officers objected. 'We're holding the *Amis*.'

Kesselring swallowed another piece of the cheap blood sausage. 'Yes, I know. They only have a clawhold on the beachhead. But the Americans regard this as a matter of prestige. They'll throw in everything they've got. You know the *Amis*. They are a very vain people. National pride is very important to them. So they'll attack and attack until we'll have to withdraw or be beaten. I don't want that to happen. I want to use their pride to give us time to pull north of Naples and let them start again to the attack.' He smiled showing those famous teeth of his, though his eyes didn't light up. He was deadly serious. 'I'll make them pay for every bit of ground they take. We'll teach the Americans that they can't walk into Europe like a bunch of damned gods and start throwing their weight about. They'll have to pay the price. As they say, *meine Herren, von nichts kommt nichts.*' He swallowed another cup of *grappa.* '*Klar*?'

'*Klar*,' they echoed as one. Just as did his footsloggers; they all had the utmost confidence in the field marshal. He always made things appear feasible, however difficult they were.

Kesselring turned to his air liaison officer, Oberst von Gluckstein. 'Well, Otto, what does the air force tell us? How far are you with your plan?'

'Almost complete, sir,' he replied promptly. He grinned. 'The enemy's in for a great surprise.'

For once Smiling Albert was not prepared to share the other officer's sense of humour. Suddenly he realized just how urgent the situation was. If he was going to save Italy for the Führer after the Italians' treachery in changing sides two months before, he had to make a success of this damned Salerno thing. 'I said we've got only four days,' he warned.

Von Gluckstein's smile vanished, He was the earnest staff officer once more. 'Understood fully, Field Marshal. And we'll do it by then. All we're waiting for is the latest Allied dispositions from our man in Bari and then we strike with every last plane available to the Luftwaffe in Italy, even artillery spotter planes, if necessary.'

Kesselring relaxed. He was pleased. For once his old service, the Luftwaffe, was not going to make a mess of things. 'Excellent. I'm pleased.' He smiled and the staff turned back to their drinks. 'By the way, what kind of a man is this fellow of yours in Bari?' he asked without too much interest and he swallowed his third piece of the cheap red sausage.

His senior aide, as was expected from senior aides,

responded immediately. 'A dark horse really, *Exzellenz*,' he barked in his old-fashioned style. 'An Italian of a kind, but a fluent German speaker. Skorzeny thinks highly of him.'

'That mountebank,' Kesselring said knowingly. 'He would. A person of no real importance then, eh?'

The aide nodded. 'But reliable and very useful, *Exzellenz*, all the same.'

'Expendable, however,' Kesselring said to himself, as if he had already dismissed the matter. He turned and took one last look at the bloody beach at Salerno, knowing he would never see it again. The soldier who had been crying over the body of the Italian child without guts was dead himself, as Kesselring knew he would be soon, if he didn't take cover immediately. He hadn't. Now he was dead, but still sagging upright, supported by his rifle dug into the wet sand, his arms outflung with the impact of the bullet which had killed him, so that he looked like some latterday Christ in a helmet, impaled on the Cross.

Kesselring told himself he was getting fanciful in his old age. It wasn't advisable for field marshals in the Greater German *Wehrmacht* to indulge in such fancies. He finished his *grappa* with a flourish and turned back to his staff. He gave them a glimpse of that famous smile of his and said, 'Gentlemen, it is time we pulled up our hind legs and left before some *Ami* gunner gets lucky and wipes out the German High Command in Italy. *Los!*'

'*Los!*' they echoed as one.

In high good humour they started to tramp back to the waiting Mercedes hidden safely behind the next knoll. Nothing could stop the disaster to come now . . .

He knew it was her even before they spoke. Hidden in the smelly doorway, he spotted her coming down the cobbled waterfront street, littered with waste and dirty scraps of paper. She was walking slowly, a basket in one hand, her head tilted to one side, almost as if she were half-expecting some sort of blow. Even in the fading light of the autumn afternoon, he could see she was pretty in that dark southern Italian fashion: olive skin, dark eyes and a beautiful, round, warm face. Suddenly he realized he was looking at a woman for the first time in years as a woman, and not as a whore whom he'd take to bed once they had agreed on the price. As if embarrassed, he felt where his left arm had once been and wondered if she would remark upon it.

'*Giorno*,' he called softly.

She didn't start. After all, this was agreed upon. Nor did she give herself away as an amateur by looking round as if she suspected she was being observed. Instead, she looked at the reflection in the glass window of the little bakery nearest to her and, satisfied that she wasn't being followed, she gave a weary smile and came toward him, handing him the empty basket. Anyone watching might have thought she was a tired housewife bringing her husband's meagre supper before he went on night shift at the docks. He looked at it, as if checking if she had provided something special off-ration and then slung it over his arm. She noticed it but didn't remark upon the fact he had only one arm. Perhaps she had been briefed on that too, judging by her reaction? They kissed in the bored working-class fashion of people who had been married for years and were only too accustomed to each other, in bed and out, and proceeded on their way. It was as if they had done this for years.

Now, as they walked side by side, trying to assess each other, the port's fetid back streets, smelling of cat's piss and ancient lecheries, were beginning to settle down for the night. Opposite them an elderly waiter in felt slippers, cigarette glued permanently to his bottom lip, was putting up the blackout shutters. A couple of workmen in faded blue overalls, who hadn't had a shave for a month, pedalled home slowly with a bottle of red wine protruding from their cheap attaché cases. A Model T Ford, run from a monstrous gas bag fixed to its roof, chugged and panted down the cobbled road, driven by two suspicious *carabinieri*. They hardly looked at the shabby couple. Even the beggar squatting in the dust, clad in the faded uniform of Mussolini's defeated African Army, didn't even attempt to ask for money. To him, obviously, they looked like all the rest of the hopeless people of no account who inhabited this run-down quarter, where soon the rats would be scavenging in the streets for whatever scraps they could find. Here everything reeked of defeat, hopelessness and failure.

The knowledge pleased Breitmeyer. It would be the ideal hiding place till the great action took place and, since he had spotted the hated outline of the *Warspite*, he was even more determined to carry out his role in the operation.

Still, preoccupied as he was with thoughts of revenge, he was intrigued by Stella Ricci. He had guessed by her accent that she belonged to the poverty-stricken south and wondered how she had become involved with German intelligence. The types the bosses in Berlin usually recruited were city folk, sophisticated people, cynics and turncoats who fought in the 'war of the shadows' for money and the like. Somehow he guessed (and later he found out he was right) her reason was connected with some ill-fated love affair. She had mentioned a child with the un-Italian name of Kurt back home in her village, living with her mother. Perhaps she was one of those unfortunate Italian girls who had been seduced by a German soldier and left with the shame and stigma of an illegimate blood 'love baby'. But Breitmeyer did not need to know if he were correct or not. So, he concentrated on the present, the best he could with a woman to whom he felt oddly attracted in a way he hadn't been since he had been a young and impressionable naval cadet, still wet behind the ears.

'Of course, there is the blackout and it covers the port, too,' she explained as they drew closer to the shabby street in which she lived. 'I have discovered that in an emergency there are places where the lighting system can be switched on – and that would, of course, illuminate the anchorage where the ships are too.

He nodded his understanding and told himself that for a country girl, she was quick and intelligent, far too intelligent, he considered, to have gotten into the dangerous business of espionage. But he kept that thought to himself. Instead he asked, 'Have you any new information that must be passed on?'

'The English warships, you have seen them?'

'Yes, I have. That is really new intelligence of great importance. The Luftwaffe must know of it so that they can provide the right kind of armour-piercing bombs for the attack.'

'They will be informed. Pietro' – she meant the wireless operator outside Bari who relayed her messages to the Germans – 'will send the news as soon as you give your approval. You are, of course, in charge now.'

He knew he was. Yet the way she made her statement made him pause. She said the words in a mixture of apparent resignation and relief, almost as if a phase of her life had come to an end and she was glad that it had done so. But what the new phase would be, he couldn't guess and indeed made no attempt to do so. For he was too concerned with the immediate future and the destruction of the *Warspite* which had now become uppermost in his thoughts.

So, he fell silent as did she. Like two humble folk, she with her bent shoulders, he with his one arm, both dressed shabbily, they disappeared down the darkening street, each wrapped in a cocoon of their own thoughts . . .

*   *   *

That same evening Captain Otto Heitman, the skipper of
the newly docked US freighter *John Bascom*, went ashore
to report. He had just crossed the Atlantic and it was part
of his first task before he enjoyed the first carefree drinks
in over two weeks, to report his arrival and hand over the
ship's manifests. As the little bumboat that had brought
him ashore passed ship after ship, he started to count them
out of idle curiosity and by the time he had sailed by the
new Liberty ship, the *John Harvey*, he had estimated there
were at least thirty of them all packed tightly together and,
as he already knew, there was another convoy due in this
very night.

The thought worried him. The harbour and its shipping would make an ideal target for an enemy aerial
attack in spite of Bari's anti-aircraft defences. The Luftwaffe
would have a field day. Even a cross-eyed Kraut pilot
couldn't miss with all those ships packed so tightly
together.

Now he pushed his way through drunken sailors and
merchant seamen of a dozen different Allied nations, ogling
the whores who strolled along the front or stood already
engaged in their business in darkened doorways, fondling
the panting, sex-starved seamen, or down on their knees
performing a highly expensive 'special'.

He went into the Port Office, going through the usual routine, telling the same old stories, cracking the usual jokes
and making the customary requests. Then, although he had
not come into the office to do so, he asked the naval
clerk, 'Hey, can I see someone in charge of defence here,
buddy?'

The young sailor was surprised. He knew his Yanks.
They were usually in and out like a shot, as if they couldn't
get at the booze and the tarts quick enough. Hesitantly he
said, 'Probably the Assistant Harbour Commandant will
see you, sir.'

'Wheel me in,' Heitman snapped, now a man with a mission.

Five minutes later he was seated over a whisky in front of a jovial, bearded lieutenant commander, who didn't seem to have a care in the world. But then, Heitman told himself, why should he? He'd found himself a home from home here in Bari. Plenty of cheap booze, a safe billet and, by the look of the Italian female clerk with her dark flashing eyes and massive bosom which threatened to pop out of her low-cut dress every time she bent over the filing cabinet, someone to keep him warm in bed of a night.

'Well,' the bearded Englishman said after a sip at his excellent whisky, 'where's the fire, Captain?'

Heitman was in no mood for long explanations. He snapped. 'Here . . . here in Bari.'

'How do you mean?'

'The way the harbour is packed, Commander. A Jerry raid as it stands now, and with another convoy coming in tonight, it'll be mass slaughter,' he answered hotly.

The Englishman took it in his stride. 'Now, now, Captain Heitman, don't you think we've got that all in hand?' He paused and waited till the Italian filing clerk had finished her job, revealing an ample portion of black silk-stockinged thigh, before adding, 'Besides, between you and me, Captain, the Jerry Luftwaffe is in no position to mount an attack on Bari. We've wiped it off the map in southern Italy and before you object,' he said hastily, 'that they have other fields from which they could fly, I can tell you they've nothing in the way of bomber fields this side of Rome. Our radar johnnies'd soon give us the wire if they took off from there.' He pushed the bottle of Scotch towards Heitman to help himself, beaming jovially at him, as if he were some harmless idiot who had to be appeased.

Heitman wasn't altogether convinced, but he had said

his piece and he knew the jovial Englishman, who had obviously found a home from home in Bari, would have thought him a crank if he persisted. So, he finished his drink and went out into the night. Far out in the anchorage he could see the riding lights of the van of the new convoy entering Bari to crowd the place even more. He shrugged and washed his hands of the matter. The English always knew best anyway – or at least they thought they did.

That same night, Petty Officer Hawkins was not so sure about the ability of his fellow Englishmen to know everything. He had just returned from indenting fresh supplies for the ageing *Warspite*, which like some old crone was beginning to fall apart at the seams – the gun hoists for 'A' turret were starting to act up, once again – when he spotted the approach of the new convoy from Algiers.

The merchantmen were making heavy weather of trying to thread their way through the packed shipping already at anchor. The tugs were sounding their sirens angrily and on the bridges of the escorting destroyers, officers were bellowing frantic instructions and corrections through their loud hailers, as freighters escaped bumping into each other in the darkness by, what seemed to a worried Hawkins, a matter of inches.

Hairless Harry who was on watch strolled over to him, hands dug deep into the pockets of his duffel coat, for it was now beginning to get very cold at night; something that none of them had expected from Italy. Under his breath he was humming in a bored fashion, 'Up came a spider, sat down besides her, whipped his old bazooka out and this is what he said, get hold o' this, bash-bash—'

'Knock off that howling, Able Seaman, 'Hawkins interjected with mock authority. 'Yer not supposed to sing when on watch, y'know.'

Hairless Harry told him what to do in a non-malicious

manner and Hawkins, also affable, retorted, 'No can do . . . I've got a double-decker bus stuffed up there already, mate.'

They relaxed. 'Do you think, Petty Officer, we can have a fly spit and a draw?' Harry asked.

Hawkins looked around. There was no one in sight on the blacked-out deck. 'Think so, Harry.'

So the two Yorkshiremen and old friends lit up, hiding the glowing ends of their cigarettes in their cupped palms, watching the confusion in the outer bay in silence for a moment, each man seemingly preoccupied. Finally Harry said, 'Did yer get a bit o' the other, mate?'

Hawkins shook his head. 'Ner. Didn't have time. The bloody old ship's falling apart agen and I was indenting for this, that and the other. Besides I was a bit off it.'

'Bit off it!' Harry exclaimed in mock surprise. 'When's a matelot off a bit o' juicy gash . . . Unless yer going a bit of funny on me.' He simpered.

'You'll be going funny in half a mo, with me boot up your slack arse!' Hawkins threatened with no real vehemence.

Harry stubbed out his cigarette and said softly (for him), 'But I know what yer mean, Jim. I don't like it.'

'What?'

'Here, this place. Don't like it a bit. Bari, they can have.'

'Might be better than where we're going,' Hawkins said.

'Yer mean Salerno?'

'Right.'

'Well, you know where you are when they're flinging shit at yer, Jim, at least. Here' – he shivered suddenly, as if attacked by a fever '– I don't know.'

Hawkins nodded but didn't respond. He stared out into the night and the tiny lights of the convoy, which was now finally seeming to find its allotted berths. But he was no longer watching the ships. Faintly he could hear the sound of aircraft engines, or so he imagined, as when he asked Hairless Harry if he had heard them as well, the big bald-headed Yorkshireman replied, 'No, can't say I did, that bloody Yankee Liberty ship was making too much of a racket.' He straightened. 'Well, better get on, Jim. Before the officer of the watch comes round. No frigging peace for the wicked, eh?'

'No frigging peace for the wicked, Harry,' Jim Hawkins agreed.

Hairless Harry disappeared and slowly silence descended upon the anchorage as the ships' engines ceased beating and the slither of the anchor chains indicated that the new convoy was finally heaving to. Yet in the new silence, Hawkins sensed a tension. Or was it in himself? A feeling of foreboding and apprehension. About what? What could happen to them, a mighty fleet tucked away safely inside this well-defended Allied port, some hundred miles away from the fighting front? After all, the war was raging now on the other side of Italy.

Still, he could not rid himself of that uneasy sensation that something terrible – he knew not what – was going to happen. He shivered abruptly and it wasn't the night cold that made him do so. It was sheer naked fear. 'Put a sock in it, Jim, for Chrissake,' he whispered to himself angrily. 'You're behaving like a frigging old tart!'

It was about then that the thick drunken voice came winging over the line of silent ships, interrupted by the sound of the cooks' galley slops being thrown over the side into the greasy oily water below.

'Momma's on the bottom . . . Poppa's on the top . . . Baby's in the crib shouting . . . Give it to her, Pop . . . Goddam Christ Almighty, Who the fuck are we? . . . We're the raiders of the night . . . WE'D RATHER FUCK THAN FIGHT . . .'

The words sung by some unknown American negro cook broke the tension. His sense of foreboding vanished. He grinned at the darkness, then yawned. It was time to turn in. Tomorrow was another day . . .

Four

Breitmeyer had not wanted to make love to the girl, Stella. He hadn't thought it right. Besides, he had felt beforehand he would have been embarrassed. With a whore it would have been different. He would have paid his money and instructed her how to do it with a one-armed man. But with a girl who was letting him lay her down on her back, take off her knickers and spread her legs so that he could fumble and thrust home his member finally, it was different.

There were so many things that he hadn't realized one needed two hands for before he had lost his. But he had soon learned it was the most intimate human actions that were the most difficult and when two people were concerned, the most embarrassing. How did you excite a woman while at the same time undoing your flies and direct a stiff penis into an excited orifice, when the woman was gasping and panting and already moving her loins back and forth excitedly, as if she were already enjoying the crazy pleasure of sexual intercourse? It was something, he had concluded since he had lost his left arm back in 1941, best left to prostitutes, who were being paid for the business and therefore had to take a man as he came, crippled or not.

Of course, it had been the bottle of whisky which had started it. 'It is a present for you.' She had offered it to him in that humble, peasant-like manner of hers (though he found out later she was anything but a dumb peasant from the back of beyond). 'I was given it –' she had lowered those beautiful liquid dark eyes of hers momentarily – 'by . . . a friend.' While he had opened it, she fussed finding two chipped glasses in the tiny room that were her quarters in a manner that he thought somehow was embarrassed.

By the light of the naked yellow bulb, hung with flypapers in the centre of the room, its only decoration holy pictures of the cloying sentimental Italian peasant style and a photograph of a boy, whom he found out later was her 'love child', they talked and talked and all the while he kept on drinking. At first they had discussed the great operation to come, for which she showed no great enthusiasm, only relief as if she couldn't get away from Bari soon enough.

Outside the port grew progressively more silent. There was a curfew in force for both military and civilians and by midnight the only sound was the solid tramp of the heavy-booted foot patrols on the cobbles outside and the slow grind of the American 'white mice' (the white-helmeted US Military Police) in their jeeps. By one, even they had vanished and, sitting there on the hard-backed wooden chains in the circle of yellow light cast by the single bulb, they might well have been the last people left alive in the whole wide world.

Some time about three, the room chilly now despite the fact that they had consumed most of the bottle of whisky and were flushed with alcohol, she told him. It had sobered him immediately, as if he had just sprung into one of the freezing glacial lakes of his South Tyrolean homeland; he had been so shocked.

She explained how she had been unable to 'make up to the *Amis*', as had been originally suggested by her control. A woman had been different and among the nurses, so her control had maintained, there was always one or two who would be that way inclined.

'You mean *lesbian*?' he had asked.

She had nodded numbly, her head bent, her raven-black hair falling and momentarily hiding her face. For a few moments he had had a vision of her naked, entwined in the grasp of another naked woman, both doing perverse, impossible things to each other: things he had been hardly able to comprehend, even if he had wanted to – which he hadn't.

Then he dismissed them firmly and, as she began to cry softly, he forgot his shock, his inhibitions, his permanent rage at the way he had been cruelly tortured and crippled by the perfidious English. He took her in his arm, whispering stupid infantile things, words he had almost forgotten, comforting her, kissing her gently and it had happened . . .

Dawn came. Outside the port was beginning to come to life once more. He blinked open his eyes. Despite the amount of whisky he had drunk the night before, he had never felt so good, so happy, so alive. Gently he eased his arm from beneath her in the tight single bed. She sighed, a silly, girlish smile playing about her lips, and had gone back to sleep almost immediately.

With pleasure, he looked down upon her. She was naked. Her body was like that of a schoolgirl, not that of a woman and mother who had a two-year-old child waiting for her in the village where she had been born. Her breasts were slight and pink-tipped, with tiny nipples while the patch of hair at her loins was faint and wispy. At that moment, she looked like a girl of fourteen, a virginal schoolkid, who could never have done the things to that *Ami* woman which she had.

'Damn,' he cursed under his breath. It was these corrupt Anglo-Americans with their superior airs once again; they corrupted and besmudged everything that they touched.

They deserved what was coming to them. He shook his head like a diver coming up for air and told himself that he shouldn't be angry. He and she would take their revenge for the past and then what had happened would be forgotten. Neither of them owed anything to the state in which they had been born and the one they were currently serving. Once this business was over, they'd escape to a new life. What kind of life that would be, he didn't quite know. But he knew, like an article of faith, that there had to be one; *there had to be!*

Thus it was that when she finally awoke to the noise of the early morning trams rumbling through the streets taking the workers to the docks and the shrill whistles heralding the start of the day's first shift, he was waiting for her with fresh coffee (courtesy of the American lesbian) and the typical aniseed-tasting buns that he had stolen out to buy with his forged bread coupons at the corner bakery. '*Alora,*' he announced, 'the signora's breakfast is served.'

Perhaps it was the only happy moment in his tortured life . . .

'All right, lads,' Petty Officer Hawkins announced. 'This is the buzz.'

The young crew of 'A' turret leaned forward eagerly, as all around them, the *Warspite* pulsated with activity. Like all young matelots, they lived on the ship's rumours or 'buzzes', unlike the old hands that Hawkins remembered from 1939 in what now seemed another age. They'd been cynics: 'Seen it, heard it, done it, forgot it' had been their motto. For them 'buzzes' had only meant fresh trouble – and danger.

'We're off!' Hawkins lowered his voice. 'Got it from the Captain's own writer. Keep it under yer tit-for-tats, but it's Salerno, as we expected.' He quelled the sudden excited chatter with his right hand. 'All right, all right, don't be a lot o' tarts. Keep it down to a frigging quiet roar.' He lowered his voice even more, glancing swiftly to left and right as if checking whether he was being overheard. 'There's more . . . another buzz, that's even more important and anyone of you lugs who blabs where he heard it, I'll have his guts for garters if I find out.' He gave them a cold smile. In fact, he was feeling quite pleased with himself. For a twenty-two-year-old recently promoted petty officer, he was beginning to sound like one of those hairy-assed old CPOs who had been in the Royal seemingly since the days of Old Nelson himself.

'It's this.' Again he paused, making them strain to hear what he was going to say next. 'After this Salerno do, we're off back to Blighty. According to the buzz, we're going to be tarted up for one last go at old Jerry.'

They were listening intently, their young faces strained and totally concentrated at that mention of Blighty.

Hawkins made the most of it. 'It'll be on D-Day. Supporting the invading troops. Once we've got the brown jobs ashore, it'll be Liberty Hall for the lads of the *Warspite*, free beer and as much hot gash as yer can manage.'

His words had their effect as he had expected they would. Their faces lit up. One of his crew wasn't convinced however. He said, 'But they'll never let the *Warspite* off the hook. In the Admiralty they're allus making lash-ups as far as the old ship is concerned. They've done it now for four years. Betcha they'll find another job for us once we've won the invasion.'

Hawkins smiled at him as if in pity. 'Get the digit outa the orifice, Meadows, for Chrissake,' he said. 'Ain't you got eyes? The old *Warspite*'s had it ain't she? She's falling apart at the frigging seams, ain't she, the poor old bitch? We'll be lucky to see her through the invasion and then, mates, it's Easy Street, believe you me.' His confident mood vanished suddenly, as he realized once again, just

119

how vulnerable this packed anchorage at Bari was. 'But let's get the fuck outa here, *toot sweet*, before anything bloody well goes wrong.' He shivered, though later he couldn't reason why.

Over half a mile away, Captain Heitman of the USS *John Bascom* was also still preoccupied with that strange feeling of foreboding that had overcome him ever since he had sailed into Bari. Now it seemed to centre on the freighter *John Harvey* anchored not far away from his own ship.

She was American and she was a fairly recently built Liberty ship, he could see that as he surveyed her now yet again. But that was about all he could tell. For the *John Harvey* was strangely closed up. Just once he had spotted someone on the bridge and then a cook throwing slops overboard to the accompaniment of the greedy shrieks of the diving gulls. There were none of the usual lazy groups of sailors playing cards on the deck or idling at the rail, enjoying the sun and their off-duty time. Even the crew's Liberty boat remained firmly attached to the side, as if the crew were not inclined or permitted to go ashore for a few hours and enjoy the coarse pleasures of Bari's red light district.

'Why?' he asked himself aloud, as he surveyed the other ship from his own bridge, talking to himself in the fashion of lonely men. What was so special about the prefabricated Liberty ship built in a couple of weeks in one of Kaiser's huge shipyards? That kind of ship was ten-a-penny these days.

In the end, Captain Heitman gave up trying to solve the puzzle – if there really was a puzzle. He told himself that he was getting as nervous about the matter as some old dame with nerves. The best he could do was to get his ship cleared and be off out to sea before whatever was going to happen – *if anything was* – did.

It was good advice, but it would come too late. Later that day, he would watch enviously as the two ancient limey battleships *Warspite* and *Valiant* started to steam slowly out of the anchorage. He knew they were sailing to battle. You didn't need a crystal ball to guess they were heading for the new front at Salerno. All the same, in the mood he was in at this moment, he wished fervently he could go with them . . .

Breitmeyer clenched his one fist with suppressed rage. It was late afternoon. The two of them had watched the English battleships leave the harbour and then he had gone with her to this place, the American lesbian's smart flat in the street opposite the US General Hospital. They had walked in silence, their mood heavy with tension. Once she had begun with: 'It's the last time, if we want to know about the emergency lighting—' But she had broken off hurriedly as she had seen the stony look on his face. They had finished the walk in silence.

Now, although he had promised her he would go straight back to the safety of her room, he had posted himself in the doorway opposite the upstairs flat with the big sign outside in English and Italian: 'OFF LIMITS TO NON-US PERSONNEL' and watched the windows, though he knew there'd be nothing to be seen. All the same, he would have gone mad, he knew it, alone in her one room, knowing what she and the Yankee pervert were up to at this moment. Indeed, in that same moment that he had said goodbye to Stella, at the door guarded by an Italian policeman, he had been overcome by the burning wish to grab her by the hand and cry, 'Damn the operation! Let's get the hell out of this awful place *now!*' But he had resisted the urge; his sense of duty and desire for revenge on the English had been too strong. Now consumed by anger, resentment and sexual jealousy, he waited and waited, praying that her ordeal would be over soon. Yet at the same time, he was assailed by a sneaking, terrible feeling that Stella might be enjoying what the pervert was now doing to her.

She wasn't!

At first she had let it happen: the usual cuddling, the excited tiny kissing, the gasping, the tongue smelling of cigarette smoke forced into her mouth and making her gag. It was to be the last time and she was prepared to accept it in order to find out what they wanted to know from the gross coarse American woman. But then, when she had started forcing strong drinks on her, as she usually did in order to 'loosen you up, kid. Relax and enjoy yourself', she had begun to worry.

The woman had gone into the bedroom saying over her fat shoulder, 'I've got a surprise for you, kid. Took me a heck of a lot of dough to get it . . . But I know you'll enjoy it. I know *I* will.' With that she had winked and disappeared inside. Stella had given a sigh of relief and had waited.

But when the woman had returned, she had been at first inclined to laugh out loud at her appearance and then she had grown frightened at the realization of what she was going to do her.

She had posed in the door of the bedroom almost triumphantly. She was totally naked, her breasts, dung-nippled and pendulous, hanging down unpleasantly. But it had not been the American's gross body which had caught Stella's attention. It had been the 'instrument' – she couldn't think of any better word for it – bobbing up and down in front of the thick thatch of black pubic hair. The only comparison that her shocked mind had been able to make was with that of a policeman's rubber club – and just as dangerous.

'What d'ya think of it, Stella?' she had breathed, eyes gleaming almost feverishly as she had posed there, the contraption of metal and rubber attached to her loins wobbling with the movement. 'I'm sure you're gonna love it, *cara mia.*'

Stella had been too frightened to speak. She was going to use that monstrous thing on her – she knew it. God, how terrible! 'But I can't . . .' The words died in her throat, as the woman clutched her suddenly very hard and she felt the cold length of that brutal instrument pressed up against her burning stomach.

'*Please . . . please!*' she cried piteously.

'You'll love it, kid. There's no man in this world that can give you same thrill I can with this . . .' Brutally the American woman had forced open her skinny legs with her knee and then she had screamed and screamed . . .

'*Melde gehorsamt,*' the Wing Commander cried, as if he were back on the parade ground, '*Geschwader vollständigt.*' The keen-looking colonel clicked his heels together harshly and touched his right hand to the gleaming black peak of his rakishly tilted cap.

'*Danke!*' General der Flieger von Richthofen acknowledged casually in the manner of senior officers who no longer need to appear zealous and full of Prussian military ardour.

He looked around the rows of eager young faces, intelligent, keen, the best the Luftwaffe could field in this fourth year of war and was pleased with what he saw. 'Please be seated, gentlemen,' he ordered. 'Smoke if you wish – and if you've got any.' He added the old soldier's phrase and as they shuffled their feet and sat down, some of them grinned. They knew where they stood with an 'old hare', a veteran like the general. After all, the dynamic little general was a scion of the same family which had once sired the legendary 'Red Baron', Germany's greatest ace of World War One.

Von Richthofen gave the pilots and observers a few

moments to settle down before starting with his instructions. 'Yesterday morning,' he announced, 'our spies tell us that the English Air Marshal *Sir* Arthur Coningham told a press conference that the Allies had total air supremacy over southern Italy.' He paused, cleared his throat, grinned and added, 'He said to the reporters present that he would regard it as a personal insult if the German Luftwaffe would attempt one single significant air attack in that area.' His grin broadened. 'Gentlemen, tomorrow we will *significantly* insult the good Sir Arthur.' He paused for laughter and he got it. After all, poor joke or not, junior officers always laughed at generals' jokes.

'Now, gentlemen,' von Richthofen continued, his face set and purposeful once more. 'Kesselring has given us twenty-four hours. We must support the Salerno operation the best we can. More –' he raised his forefinger like some pious Lutheran pastor of his East Prussian homeland delivering a strict warning – 'support it to the utmost.'

There was a murmur of agreement among the listening pilots. Twice the Army had denied them the chance to play a satisfactory role in ops in Italy: once at the outset of the invasion of Sicily in July and then two months later in the Allied landings in southern Italy. Now they were eager to show their mettle

'*Jawohlja!*' someone cried with a burst of enthusiasm.

'We must create chaos in Bari and before the Allies have recovered, we shall tackle the English navy's capital ships, which we have just heard are on the way to Salerno.' Von Richthofen loked around the circle of eager, hot-eyed young faces and knew instinctively these Luftwaffe fanatics, burning for some desperate glory, wouldn't let him down even if it cost their own lives. 'Those capital ships *must* and *will* be sunk. How, you ask? I shall tell you!'

'*Hoch . . . hoch!*' Carried away by sudden youthful enthusiasm, they yelled. A few, the Nazis among the aircrews, even sprang to their feet. Standing to attention, right hand extended rigidly, they bellowed, '*Sieg Heil . . . Sieg Heil!*'

Patiently von Richthofen waited till the tumult had begun to calm down, a faint knowing smile playing on his hard aristocratic face. Already in the distance he could hear the faint throb of the engines of the plane which would take part in this surprise demonstration. He continued to wait, while his staff officers frowned professionally at the young pilots and observers until finally even the ardent Nazis sat down and started to look around as if they were checking that no one had noticed their sudden outburst.

'*Meine Herren*,' von Richthofen commenced. 'I have one small matter to show you before you depart this room for your individual briefings. I would be obliged to you, if you would come to the windows on this side of the building so I can demonstrate.'

Puzzled but obedient, the officers pushed back their chairs yet again and did as they were ordered.

Von Richthofen waited till they had all found a place and then said, 'Regard the plane at fifteen hundred hours if you would.'

As one, like intrigued spectators at a pre-war tennis match, the assembled air crew clicked their heads to the right. There, a tiny spot on the mild blue autumn sky was slowly turning into the well-remembered shape of a twin-engined Junkers 88 fast bomber. But even the slowest pilot recognized that there was something strange about the outline of the workhorse of the German bomber arm. There appeared to be something mounted in the upper fuselage of the Junkers.

Von Richthofen spoke to the nearest staff officer. Immediately he whirled the handle of the field telephone standing on the table next to him. He spoke. It was one word, a curt '*jetzt!*'.

125

Suddenly the Junkers lurched upwards, as if it had suddenly struck a thermal. It rose at least twenty metres. The jump upwards was followed by a flash of light. Next moment the spectators saw the reason for the plane's sudden change of altitude. The load, whatever it was, had detached itself, from the carrier.

They gasped as one. The load had turned into a small plane with an apparent life of its own, but it was unlike any plane they had seen before. It was squat with stubby wings, though it had a large rudder, and it was obvious that it was pilotless.

Even before they asked, von Richthofen enlightened them. 'Remote-controlled, electrically,' he explained. 'Steered by an observer next to the pilot in the Junkers. Now watch.'

Excited and intrigued at this new secret weapon – one of the many that the Führer had recently promised would eventually blast the Western Allies off the face of the world – they watched open-mouthed as the glider bomb, for that was what it would be later called when the secret was out, came lower and lower. It was clear that it was being controlled for it came down in a series of strange zig-zags in a manner that no human pilot could achieve.

'Observe the target at ten hundred,' von Richthofen announced. 'Between those two groves of olive trees.'

They switched their gaze once more and saw the red painted target: a large piece of hessian, some two metres square, attached to a trolley which was moving very slowly, though it moved at sufficient speed to make it difficult to hit. The pilots knew that from personal experience.

Von Richthofen snapped something at the staff officer at his side. He whirred the handle of the field telephone once more. His contact made, again he uttered two words only: 'Attack . . . Destroy!'

Almost immediately the glider bomb changed course. Now it began coming down at a steep angle – fast. Above it, its control plane, the Junkers, flew higher and higher, till it was a barely perceivable dot in the sky. At that height, the mesmerized watching pilots knew, it would be damnably difficult for the enemy flak to knock it out of the sky.

'Three thousand pounds of high explosive,' von Richthofen broke in. His voice reflected the growing excitement of the spectators. 'Capable of penetrating at least three armoured decks of the average Tommy battleship—' The rest of his words were drowned by a tremendous explosion. The target vanished. The rail upon which the trolley had run disappeared too in that very same instant. To either side the olive trees were lashed back and forth with the blast. They scattered their leaves like silver rain. And then from the steaming new crater which looked like the work of some monstrous mole, smoke started to rise straight into the sky in a dark mushroom.

Von Richthofen, highly pleased with himself and the effect of his surprise demonstration, turned to his officers and said simply, 'The end of the *Warspite*, gentlemen.'

Now that the battleships had gone, the port settled down for the night. Those who had managed to get overnight shore leave filled the bars and brothels of the waterfront, drinking and whoring. The Italians, those who were not able to buy on the thriving black market, settled down in the poorly lit hovels to eat an evening meal of cheap polenta and pasta washed down, if they were lucky, with sour wine, well watered down already before they had bought it.

Outside the streets, apart from the noise made by drunken carousing sailors and GIs – the new millionaires of occupied Italy – the city started to grow quieter and quieter. The trams had ceased running, the docks had shut down for the night and the convoys, which had run back and forth had grown fewer. As yet the Allied-Italian patrols had not commenced. It was too early to start cleaning up the human wreckage which eventually would flood out from the bars and brothels.

In her one room the two sat in an awkward silence. They avoided looking at each other directly, but whenever he did manage to steal a covert glance at Stella he could see that she was still hurting from whatever the damned American lesbian had done to her – he daren't ask. Several, times, too, she had gone out to the outside privy with the customary pail of water and by straining his ears, he could hear her moaning piteously. But again he dared not say anything. He felt that if he did, his rage might just boil over and he'd explode. And this was no time to explode.

By now they knew from their mysterious 'pianist', the radio operator Pietro, that their information had been received at Luftwaffe HQ and neither needed to be clairvoyant to know that the bombers would descend upon Bari either this coming dawn or the one afterwards. The German High Command could not afford to wait much longer. It was for that reason that the two of them were waiting in this narrow little room, trying to bottle in their hatred and resentment so that they would be ready to carry out their part of the great plan once the signal for the impending raid was given.

Again she returned from the privy. She looked wan and dejected. Carefully she placed the pail down in its allotted place next to the door and sat down stiffly. She was in pain, he could see that and there were still deep black bags under her eyes so that she looked sick and unhealthy. 'What time is it?' she asked wearily for the umpteenth time.

He told her. But he waited for a reaction from her in vain. It was as if, since her last meeting with the lesbian, she had sealed herself off from intimate contact with him; as if she were afraid to speak any more than, say, asking the time in case she aroused an outbreak of passion, temper or a lust to kill.

Sink the Warspite

Inwardly he sighed and wished it would all start. He couldn't stand this internal tension much longer. He lapsed into a sulky silence, while she squirmed on her hard chair, sunk into her own gloomy thoughts, wondering if she would ever escape the misery of war . . .

By two that night, the two of them, as if in response to some unspoken command, began packing the carpetbags that would contain their meagre escape kit. The home-made bags would be slung over their shoulders while they carried out their part in the attack and then they would head out of Bari immediately, hoping to merge with other civilians who would undoubtedly panic and run. Thus, before the Anglo-American military authorities would have time to start organizing checks, they'd be out in the open countryside.

As they packed the hard polenta, a loaf she had managed to obtain off the bread ration and two cans of spam that the lesbian had given her, they spoke little, only what was necessary. Yet even so, Breitmeyer felt that the unspoken bond between them had been re-established. They would go together and leave the war behind. Perhaps they would find refuge in the mountain village where her son was being taken care of? He didn't know for certain. But what he did know one hundred per cent, as if the fact was graven in tablets of stone: they would stick together now. They were victims of the war, abandoned to their fate. Yet if they stayed together, the crippled agent knew implicitly, they'd survive, perhaps even make a new life for themselves.

Thus it was, their packing finished, sitting silently opposite each other in the circle of sickly yellow light, they heard the faint hesitant drone of a plane out to sea and realized instinctively that their time had come. Wordlessly he stretched out his one hand to her. Stella took it, also without a word. He pressed hard. She returned the pressure.

Again no words were exchanged, but the slow tears which began to course down her pale, sick, beautiful face told him all he needed to know. Suddenly, he was happy . . .

Captain Heitman of the *John Bascom* couldn't sleep. Normally he wasn't very sensitive: rough-tough skippers of deep-water freighters usually weren't. But ever since sailing into Bari, he had been apprehensive. More than once he had snapped at himself, 'For Chrissake, Otto, don't be such a goddam Nervous Nelly!' But it had not worked. Even the half a bottle of good Scotch he had consumed since midnight hadn't. He was as wideawake and jittery as ever.

For the umpteenth time he looked at his watch as he stretched out on the tight confines of his bunk, the only sound the tread of the deck watch on the steel plates above, and somewhere far, far away, the faint hum of an airplane's motor.

It seemed to take him a long time to notice the sound – perhaps it was the effects of the Scotch? He frowned as he noted it. He couldn't understand why at first he was doing so – again due to the whisky. Then it dawned upon him. It was highly unlikely that a plane would be flying over the crowded habour at this time of the night when it couldn't be easily identified. There were ships in the anchorage from half a dozen Allied nations. All carried ack-ack manned by half-trained seamen gunners, who could be assumed to be very trigger-happy. Let an unidentified plane cross the massed ships and let one nervous gunner begin firing and the whole goddam fleet would be popping away as if this was the Fourth of July. Now he began to concentrate on the low sinister buzz of the unknown plane's engine.

But not for long.

Like a sharp dagger being plunged startlingly and surprisingly into his ribs, the cry rang out just above his head on the deck.

'Skipper . . . skipper . . . I see a flare!'

He dropped the glass. It shattered on the deck. He pulled back the little blackout curtain from the cabin's sole porthole. An icy-white glacial light flooded the round sphere of glass momentarily. He gasped. There could be no mistake. This was the Krauts!

Hurriedly he flung himself out of the bunk. He pulled on his boots and jacket, the pockets stuffed with his survival gear, and panting already, he was clattering up the companionway and on to the bridge moments later, his ears already attuned to the sound of other engines coming closer and closer.

'Where?' he cried, about to grab the lookout's night glasses. There was no need. To starboard the whole horizon was lit up an unreal glistening white as more flares exploded and hung in the night, sky. 'Christ Almighty!' he yelled and then ordered, 'Sound the air-raid sirens at—'

But even as he commanded the warning, whistles, klaxons, sirens took up their dire wail all over the fleet. There was no denying it. The Germans were coming in for the attack – and in strength. This night they were out to destroy the Allied fleet, come what may . . .

Five

T rying not to panic and run, the two of them edged
their way down the dark corridor, stinking of ether,
disinfectant and human misery. Every now and again the
light of the flares stabbed its length to reveal that it was
empty, something for which Breitmeyer was glad. For
if he were discovered inside the US hospital, he knew
he'd be arrested at once; after his imprisonment on the
Warspite two years before, he had no illusions about the
Anglo-Americans. They'd soon torture his reason for being
here out of him. With his hand, he pressed the butt of the
little Biretta; it comforted him.

So far no bombs had dropped and even the sirens had
not sounded the air-raid warning on the shore itself. But
it was clear what was soon to come. The shrilling of the
sirens and the shrieking ships' klaxons made that obvious
enough. Once the Luftwaffe raiders could really pin-point
their objective, all hell would be let loose. That was why
they had to hurry, complete their task and get out of the
hospital before the balloon went up.

They slipped around another corner in the long dark
corridor. Ahead a faint light glowed. It indicated the
operating theatre, now not in use, fortunately. The casualties
from the front had ceased, but, Breitmeyer told himself
grimly, it wouldn't be long before the hospital would be
flooded with casualties. This time they would be coming
from closer to home – Bari itself.

133

'To the right,' she whispered. 'The door, you see it?'

He nodded his understanding. It was the generator room. It was intended, in the main, for the operating theatre. If the latter place lost power and the emergency lighting wasn't sufficient, and they knew it wasn't, the full power had to be turned on. Breitmeyer gave a malicious smile at the thought. And when the full power was turned on, he said to himself, it illuminated half the front part of the harbour, as it was attached to the city's general power. Then the Luftwaffe raiders would have all the illumination they needed.

'Here, take this,' he hissed and handed her the little Italian automatic. 'I'm going to force the door now. Stand guard.'

She didn't speak, but took the pistol hesitantly.

He grunted as he placed the cold chisel underneath the lock. He exerted all the strength of his powerful right arm which he had trained to do the work of two. Nothing happened. He cursed. He couldn't spend all night at the job. Outside, the noise of the prowling German bombers grew louder and louder. Soon a nervous gunner would open fire blind and the hospital personnel would be tumbling out of their cots to run to their duty positions. They'd be spotted.

He took another deep breath. Again he exerted all his strength. At his forehead, his veins stood out like steel wires. His eyes bulged with the strain. There was a crack. The catch was beginning to give. He kept at it. Somewhere further down the dark corridor he thought he heard steps. Beside him the Italian girl started. But there was no time to worry. It was now or never. Another creak. He exerted the last of his strength. The noise of metal rending. Next instant the door sagged. He'd done it!

Panting, as if he had just run a great race, he grabbed the door. Burning pains ran up his arm; his muscles were on fire. Still, he had strength enough to jerk down the switch. In an instant, the corridor was flooded with brilliant white light, followed moments later by voices shouting in alarm and someone crying angrily, 'For God's sake, douse that goddam light!'

They waited no longer. In moments the whole hospital would be alerted and the guards, American and Italian, who ran the place's security would be turning out from their makeshift barracks in the grounds to discover what was happening. They had to make a run for it while confusion still reigned and the place wasn't sealed off. 'Come on,' he cried urgently, 'let's go!' He slung his carpet bag and started running.

Stella needed no urging. She knew the danger they were in. Still holding the little Italian automatic, she darted along with him, both of them clinging to the tiled wall, running all out now. Everywhere doors were being flung open. Orders and counter-orders were rapped out. Someone was shrilling a whistle. It merged with the first wail of the air-raid sirens outside. Now all hell was breaking loose, and even as he concentrated on getting himself and Stella out of the hospital before it was too late, Breitmeyer realized that they had only a matter of minutes left before the place was sealed off. 'Keep going!' he yelled, as she started to flag. 'Don't weaken, Stella.' He grabbed her hand and with all his strength, started to drag the sick girl with him . . .

'Battle stations!' Captain Heitman bellowed, as the first ack-ack guns started to thunder. Scarlet flames stabbed the sky to reveal the dark shapes of the German bombers coming in in V-formations of three, splitting up as they approached to take on individual targets.

As his half-dressed crew, tugging on helmets and anti-flash gear, tumbled out of their bunks and on to the deck of the *John Bascom* to take on the challenge, Heitman shaded his eyes against the glare of the lights on the jetty which had gone on for some reason, despite the stringent blackout regulations, and were outlining the silhouettes of the ships in a stark dramatic black.

The attackers were twin-engined Junkers 88s and, as they came in, they were dropping a silver rain of aluminium strips first. Heitman knew why. It was the same trick the RAF bombers used. It confused enemy radar. 'Christ on a crutch!' he cursed, 'this is going to be a massacre!'

It was, but at that moment an angry frustrated Captain Otto Heitman didn't realize – and couldn't even in his wildest dreams – just how bad that massacre was going to be. The first Junkers of the nearest V of bombers was peeling off and heading straight for the mysterious *John Harvey*, which was going to be the cause of the tragedy to come.

Now the sinkings started. Within five minutes the *John Harvey* was hit. Straddled by a stick, it seemed to a gaping Heitman that she might just escape, as the Liberty ship was flung from side to side like a kid's toy ship by the blast. But the US freighter was out of luck. The third bomb of the stick struck the *John Harvey* squarely midships. Heitman groaned and felt almost physical pain himself as she disappeared momentarily in a burst of black smoke, tinged with angry cherry-red flame, with her radio mast tunbling down in a series of angry blue sparks. An instant later the Junkers was soaring into the blazing sky and the mysterious freighter was well and truly ablaze.

Heitman realized the danger to his own ship. Frantically he rang the telegraph. 'Mac,' he yelled to the engineer below, 'for fuck's sake raise steam . . . we've got to get outa here . . . *NOW!*'

But already it was too late. The second Junkers was now sneaking in, heading for the *John Harvey*'s other close neighbour, the US ship *John L Motley*, which for some reason hadn't brought its machine guns and ack-ack into play. It was an easy target for the Junkers, skidding across the anchorage at mast-height. The twin-engined bomber headed straight for the defenceless ship. At the very last moment, the pilot jerked back his stick. It soared into the burning sky, displaying its ugly blue belly, in order to gain bombing height. A moment later ugly little black eggs started to tumble from its open bomb bays in lethal profusion – and the Junkers simply couldn't miss.

The *John L Motley* was hit straight away. The stick ran the length of the freighter. Boats splintered like match-wood. Masts tumbled down. Her stack exploded. The bridge disappeared into a sea of angry scarlet flame. Within seconds the US ship was listing heavily to port, flames everywhere, panic-stricken seamen, their clothes already ablaze, casting themselves into the water, which itself was ablaze, too, with oil pouring from the ship's ruptured tanks.

Heitman turned away in utter dismay. Next moment the *John L Motley* exploded, throwing him against the bridge as if propelled by some gigantic fist. He crumpled to the deck just as the explosion started its chain reaction, spreading to the *John Harvey* and causing her, too, to explode a second later. Great clouds of thick yellow dense smoke started to pour from her burning holds the next instant . . .

'Stella – *you!*' the cry in English stabbed into the Italian girl's guts as if someone had shoved a razor-sharp stiletto into them. She stopped dead. Just behind, at the corner of the long corridor, Breitmeyer stumbled to a halt, gasping for breath. 'What in heaven's name are you doing here at the hospital at this time?'

The lesbian stood, arms folded across her lumpy hanging bosom in a hospital dressing gown at the top of the corridor, staring hard at the girl, with the one-armed man almost concealed behind her.

For a long moment, Stella could not reply. Behind her Breitmeyer, his mind racing frantically, was rooted to the ground, too, unable, it seemed, to react.

'Well,' the lesbian demanded. 'Don't I deserve an explanation . . . and who's this dago behind you? What's he doing here as well?' Her ugly yellow face contorted abruptly. 'Why, you damned bitch . . . you and the dago have been stealing from the hospital, haven't you? Behind my back—' She coughed suddenly, as the first yellow wisps of smoke filtered silently down the corridor. But she didn't seem to notice it. Instead she rasped, face flushing now with anger, 'Now, you just stay there and tell the wop to do the same. I'm going to call the military police. We'll soon get to the bottom of this.' She turned abruptly and the front of her loose gown flew open to reveal the ugly body beneath with its animal-like thatch of dark hair at the loins and the deep red marks made by that dreadful thing she had used on Stella so cruelly.

The Italian girl gasped.

The lesbian took the sound for some sort of attempt on the Italian girl's part to apologize, perhaps beg for mercy. 'No!' she snapped harshly, too angry to cover that ugly naked body, 'you have abused my trust when I have done all this for you—' She broke off, as again she was forced to cough. 'Goddamit,' she said thickly and, hawking, spat on the floor like some common working man, who knew no better.

The movement seemed to break the spell. Just in the same instant that Breitmeyer had pulled himself together and was prepared to rush the American woman before she did sound the alarm, a deadly pale Stella raised the little automatic and pointed it at the lesbian.

'*Stella!*' he cried.

Too late!

The automatic barked. The little gun jerked upwards.

But at that range, Stella couldn't miss. The lesbian was slammed back against the wall, her ugly face abruptly drained of blood. She looked down at the sudden blood-red hole bored into her stomach in absolute disbelief, as if it wasn't conceivable that this could be happening to *her*. 'You.' She tried to raise her hand, which trembled violently, as if she wished to point it in accusation at Stella. But the strain was too much. She just couldn't manage it. She gave a sigh. Slowly her body started to slither down the white-tiled wall, trailing a smear of bright red blood behind it.

Breitmeyer reacted at last. 'Come on,' he cried urgently. He tugged the automatic from Stella's nerveless fingers. He nudged her hard with his shoulder. 'Move!' he cried brutally.

She moved. Behind them the lesbian sank into the yellow mist which was now beginning to cover the corridor floor. Already her naked flesh was starting to bubble and erupt in blisters nauseatingly. Slowly she began to die, choking in her own fluids . . .

The attack lasted twenty minutes. Totally surprised as they were by the Luftwaffe, the Allied air forces weren't able to get a fighter into the air before it was all over. The result was a disaster for Allied shipping. Indeed, it was the worst seaport catastrophe that the Allies had suffered since Pearl Harbor, two years before.

In the end, seventeen ships were sunk or were sinking. Another five were blazing furiously and it didn't seem likely they could be saved. Ninety thousand tons of supplies were at the bottom of the habour or destroyed. But that was only the start. There was worse, much worse to come

Unknown to the authorities then, it was the *John Harvey* which was going to cause all the trouble. Sinking rapidly, its hull ripped open by the German bombs it began to leak its secret and deadly cargo, which had been ordered to Europe by no less a person than the President of the United States, Franklin D. Roosevelt himself. It started to mingle with the hundreds of tons of escaped oil which now floated on the debris-littered surface of the shattered harbour. Thus it formed a deadly witches' brew that reeked strongly of ripe garlic. This was not an unusual smell in Italy. But even the local workmen, rushing to the aid of the stricken ships, had never smelled garlic that strong before. Now this strange garlic-smelling mist began to roll right towards the centre of Bari itself.

By now, the Italian city was in turmoil as the hundred German bombers which had taken part in the surprise raid winged their way out to sea and the flak guns fell silent one by one. The terrified citizens, picking up their pathetic bits and pieces, rushed into the streets; some in their panic were virtually naked, too. Old people wailing for assistance were guided by barefoot urchins. Others tapped their way down the burning streets with improvised canes made of broom handles. There were dead everywhere in the blood-filled gutters. Others had been blown into the skeletal trees of the great avenues and hung there in pieces like grotesque pieces of human fruit. All was chaos, terror, panic.

Breitmeyer fought to keep his head. He held on to the girl for all he was worth. She was still in shock. The death of the lesbian had brought her to the very edge of a breakdown. Time and time again he exerted full pressure on her hand to keep going. At times he knew he was inflicting pain upon Stella. It didn't matter. Once they had cleared this mad place, he would let her rest and recover.

They stumbled with the rest of the mob down a bombed, brick-littered street. A dead woman lay in the dirty gutter. Her skirts had been flung back by the blast, her legs spread in obscene invitation. A metre away a nearly naked baby lay, too, dead as well. Perhaps it was her child. Stella

140

groaned and swayed, as if she might faint at the sight. He pressed his nails cruelly into her arm. Before they got out of Bari, he told himself, they'd see enough dead men, women *and* children. Bombs made no distinction between age and sex. 'Come on,' he commanded thickly, for suddenly bitter vomit had risen in his throat.

The bottom half of the dead baby's body was covered with what looked like a brownish-red tan. But that wasn't the horror of the sight. It was the fact that the strange-coloured skin was beginning to come off in strips and at the base of the dead baby's loins, his penis was beginning to swell to adult size with the scrotum following suit. 'God in heaven,' he cursed thickly, mouth full of bile, which was threatening to choke him. 'In three devils' names, what's going on?' They stumbled on, no longer speaking, fighting the mob, both working to an unspoken agreement that they had to get out of this place of death and horror before it was too late . . .

For many it was already too late. Everywhere, those afflicted were beginning to die. In convulsions. They coughed up their lungs in bits and pieces. The hundreds and then thousands of civilians and soldiers who managed to fight their way into the city's hospitals were in no great pain at first. But most of them were in bad shock. Their skin, at first, was cold and clammy and glistening with perspiration. Their blood pressure was abnormally low too.

In the beginning the doctors and nurses attending, to the constant stream of casualties (even the hospital's VD wards were full of these strangely injured patients) were not too worried. But soon they were. They didn't respond to treatment. Indeed, even the lightly injured seemed to get steadily worse. There was the strange change of colour that Breitmeyer had noticed. Then the patients' eyesight started to fail. By evening most of them would be blind. Now the patients started to panic and had to be restrained. Not only were some of them going blind, but most of the men were losing their manhood, as their penises swelled and burst open like overcooked sausages.

By mid-morning the hospitals were too swamped by casualties to manage. Besides, the mostly young doctors and nurses had never seen cases like this before. Despite the fact that the Salerno front had now burst wide open, with the last bloody battle raging on the beach before Smiling Albert pulled back, the authorities commandeered the surviving ships at Bari to take as many casualties as possible away to be treated elsewhere. But only the military casualties. The hundreds of Italains also stricken by this mysterious plague-like illness, were left to fend – and mostly die – for themselves in Bari. And both the military and civilian victims carried that strange odour of strong garlic.

Now the refugees from the city were out in the fields, limping along the roads and tracks, not knowing or caring where they went, as long as it was away from Bari. Children sobbed with fear, hopping along on their wounded legs, swollen, and with the strangled bronzed flesh hanging from them in strips. Women, eyes bulging out of their ashen faces under newly white hair, screamed silently. Some cradled their dead babies in their arms, fighting off any attempt to take them away. Old men, trying to retain their febrile manhood, coughed and choked until they could cough no more and, slumping to the wayside ditches, coughed up the last of their bloodied lungs.

Breitmeyer wasn't a fanciful person, but as he viewed this doleful procession of death, it seemed to him like some medieval Gothic woodcut of the Black Death, the characters trying to escape from the skeletal Grim Reaper, from whom, however, there was no reprieve.

That afternoon Stella died. He had cradled her the best he could in a nest of blankets in the drainage ditch by the roadside. She was blind by now and her skin had turned that red-brown colour. But she seemed beyond pain. Occasionally she gave a soft moan, but that was all. She simply lay there, breathing a little harder than normal, calm and unflurried, as if she knew she was going to die and was awaiting death with good grace.

More than once, almost as if he were speaking to himself, he asked, 'Why you, Stella, darling? . . . Why not me?'

But there as no answer to that overwhelming question.

Slowly he rose to his feet. He knew he ought to have buried her. It was the correct thing to do. But why did it matter to place dead ones under the earth now? It was only a way of hiding them from the view of others. Let those who still lived see the work of their fellow human beings. Let the world know of man's inhumanity to man.

Breitmeyer glared at the burning sky behind them, his eyes filled with an undying, perhaps even mad, unreasoning hatred. 'You'll pay,' he swore. 'By God, all of you will pay!'

He turned. His face hollowed out to a scarlet death's head by the flames of the harbour, he pressed his trembling hand to his heart. It was as if he were making a binding, unbreakable convenant with himself. *'You'll pay,'* he choked.

Without another look at the body crumpled in the ditch, he started walking to the west, his eyes full of madness . . .

BOOK FOUR

D-Day
June 6, 1944

'Twas on a summer's day – the sixth of June:
I like to be particular in dates . . .
They are a sort of post-house, where the Fates
Change horses, making history change its tune,
Then spur away o'er empires and o'er states . . .

Lord Byron, Don Juan

One

'Mustard gas,' the American petty officer said, voice still a little hoarse with the long-term after-effects. 'At least that's the latest scuttlebutt.'

Petty Officer Joe Hawkins, formerly of the *Warspite*, said, 'Christ, I thought they only used gas – the Jerries, I mean – in the last war.'

Petty Officer Al Gore, formerly of the USS *President Barr*, gave his lop-sided grin. 'Yeah, and it wasn't the Jerries. It was our own people. That's what the man says, at least.'

'Keep moving,' the big burly CPO in charge of the volunteers urged. 'Come on, me lucky lads. Plenty more room inside. 'Obediently the re-mustered petty officers from half a dozen Allied nations shuffled forward to where the emergency board was sitting in the examination room of Portsmouth's Haslar Naval Hospital.

'How do you mean, Al?' Hawkins asked, feeling his wounded thigh beginning to throb once more, painfully. The wound itself had healed weeks ago, ever since they had shipped him back from Naples to England at the turn of the year. But it was the standing, waiting in this long queue of volunteers, which was putting a strain on the leg. Still, he told himself, when he had his five minutes in front of the board, he'd have to smile and look confident and as if he could run ten miles before breakfast.

'According to the scuttlebutt, our guys discovered a

stockpile of German gas when they surrendered in North Africa back in the spring of 1943. So that Jew, Roosevelt, in the White House' – there was a sudden bitterness in Al's normally friendly, easy-going voice – 'decided we ought to have gas in the Italian theatre – just in case. So, what does he do, the bird-brain we call our President?' I'll tell you. He ships a freighter full of the stuff, the *John Harvey*, to Bari and when the Krauts attack, nobody knows a goddam about it.' He shrugged eloquently. 'She goes up, nothing's done because nobody knows about the ship's cargo and we all go blind or lose the family jewels.'

He grabbed the front of his pants dramatically and the red-faced CPO growled, 'If you Yanks want to wank, off yer go to the heads. We're having none of that here. We're British, you know.' For some reason known only to himself, the old petty officer guffawed heartily.

Al wasn't offended. Her smiled, the bitterness gone from his pale sick face. Instinctively, Hawkins knew *he* wouldn't get through the board. 'So we weren't even close to the *John Harvey*, but we took some of the casualties aboard and we were ordered to sail *toot sweet* for Taranto or somewhere like that. By the time we were halfway there, most of us were blind, God knows how we made harbour!' He shrugged. 'I was one of the lucky ones. Despite that Jew in the White House, I survived.'

Jim Hawkins didn't quite understand the references to the 'Jew in the White House' and the American's attack on his own president, but then the Yanks were funny altogether, and besides Al had had a tough time of it with his eyes. When he had first met him four weeks before, the Yank had still been tapping his way about with a white cane. Now he and Al were both hoping to be boarded to Combined Ops and take part in the war again – even if it was only going to be a small part. But both of them had a score to settle with old

Jerry, after Bari in the Yank's case, and his own off
Salerno . . .

The previous day they had sailed back and forth just off
the Italian coast, pounding the German positions with their
great 15-inch guns. The buzz on the gun deck was that the
Yanks were about to pack in and evacuate their beachhead
and so the *Warspite* had been forced to take risks that she
wouldn't normally have done. Everywhere there had been
flames and fire and furious explosions. On the heights the
massed German 88s pounded the Yanks, cowering in their
beachhead foxholes, remorselessly. Their casualties had
mounted rapidly and even the matelots, unused to land
warfare, could tell from the red and yellow signal flares
sailing into the smoke-filled air all along the narrow strip
of Allied-held beach, that the 'brown jobs' were taking bad
casualties.

It was this fact that must have motivated the *Warspite*'s
skipper to take her in so close. Indeed at that range they had
become target for the enemy 88s on the heights. But not for
long. With the Captain of Marines risking his neck to spot
for the *Warspite* on the beach itself, the massive 15-inchers
took one after another enemy gunpit out of action. Each
time there was a hit the sweating blackened gunners,
looking like medieval men-at-arms in their helmets and
flash gear, raised a brave cheer. All the same, they knew,
even Hairless Harry, the risk they were running. One
lucky shell from the German side and the ready locker
ammunition could go up in a furious explosion and then
it would be the 'Old Lady's' turn to suffer. As Jim Hawkins
worried that fatal afternoon off Salerno, he little realized
just how gravely the *Warspite* was about to suffer.

It was about two that afternoon, after the *Warspite* had
withdrawn slightly from the beachhead, the main German
threat beaten off for the time being at least. The gunners

relaxed and those who could grabbed the luke-warm cocoa the cooks brought up from the galleys and the thick wads of greasy corned beef between stale white bread. The 'old heads', meanwhile, secretly consumed what remained of their saved rum ration, telling themselves it was strictly against King's Regulations to do so, but what the hell? If they were going to die, they were going to do so nice and tiddly.

So as they attempted to snatch a couple of minutes of respite and relaxation from the incessant bombardment, the lookouts were momentarily surprised by the formation of twelve, black-painted Messerschmitts that suddenly skidded in from the smoke-shrouded beach. They raced towards the *Warspite* at mast-height. Their prop wash churned the sea a yard or two below into a thick white fury. Almost immediately their multiple cannon started to chatter. A furious white hail of 20mm cannon shells hissed towards the great battleship. On the deck men fell everywhere. Electric sparks from exploding shells zipped the length of the hull. Carley floats exploded. Lifeboats were shredded to wood pulp. In an instant a furious battle ensued as the weary, begrimed gunners took up the bloody challenge once again.

'Christ on a frigging crutch!' Hairless Harry moaned as they raced to take over their turret once more. 'Ain't there no frigging peace for a frigging sailor?'

'Keep yer hair on, Harry,' someone cried and Hairless Harry yelled as he slammed into the gun-layer's position, eye automatically adjusting to the firing telescopic sight. 'If I find out who said that, I'll paste him.' But Hairless Harry's days of pasting people were about over.

So the *Warspite* fought back as the Messerschmitts zoomed back and forth like a flight of angry hornets, cannon blazing, punching death and destruction at the steel colossus. The sorely plagued *Warspite* now had her decks littered with empty shell and cartridge cases and those still figures which would never move again.

It was in the midst of this furious attack, which the *Warspite*'s crew realized only afterwards was a feint, that the top lookouts started to sing out their warnings, 'Aircraft to starboard red . . . zero . . . ! As one, the bridge staff swung up their glasses. Way up in the sky there were three black dots visible, ploughing straight ahead in what seemed a course that would take them well away from the embattled warship.

In the midst of his staff, the skipper of the *Warspite*, Captain Packer, breathed a sigh of relief. 'Looks, gentlemen, as if some poor old other basket's going to get that lot—' He never finished the sentence.

In that same instant, the three black dots turned vertically. As one they dived, gathering speed at an amazing rate as they headed straight for the *Warspite*. At the same time the Messerschmitts scattered, breaking to left and right in crazy formations as if they could not get away from the scene of the action soon enough.

Automatically, for some reason he couldn't fathom later, Captain Packer started to count off the seconds as the three planes zoomed in at a terrifying rate: 'Six . . . five . . . four . . .'

With a hellish explosion, the first glider bomb, for that was what it was, struck the ship. It penetrated deck after deck. It went through the *Warspite*'s massive deck armour like a hot blade through butter. Finally, six decks down, it struck the Number Four Boiler Room and exploded.

A series of massive shakes seized the *Warspite*. On the deck, the lookouts grabbed frantically for stanchions. The whole ship vibrated madly as she started to lose power, while on the bridge the various warning lights began to flash an urgent red. The ship was in serious trouble already.

But there was more to come . . .

A handful of seconds later, the second of the new secret weapons splashed into the water a hundred yards away from the damaged *Warspite*'s midships. Cheers resounded when it seemed it had apparently missed but these died on the deck crew's lips suddenly as a massive shock made the 30,000 ton battleship shake like a kid's toy. Bursting under water, it was followed almost at once by the third near miss which had exactly the same impact on the now gravely damaged *Warspite*.

Below decks all was chaos. Men were flung from bulkhead to bulkhead. They caromed from side to side like billiard balls. Gear showered down upon their heads. In the engine room dials shattered. Glass flew everywhere, dealing the stokers terrible lacerating wounds. Steel fixtures snapped as if they were made of matchwood. Steam started to escape in scalding hot jets. Stokers screamed like hysterical women as it seared the flesh from their naked upper bodies in great ugly stripes. Here and there their skins bubbled and popped and then burst in pink eruptions. A petty officer clambered blindly up to report to the bridge, his face dripping down on to his chin like red molten sealing wax. All was horror and sudden, terrible death.

Slowly but inevitably, the *Warspite* started to lose power. One boiler room was completely flooded already. Before long the other four out of five would be in the same pathetic state. For a few frightening minutes the *Warspite*'s captain thought that the three-thousand-pound flying bomb had broken the ship's back and that her mast would soon come crashing down to her deck. But the chief engineer soon reassured him that wasn't the case. Otherwise, his information was not good. All steam was lost and the *Warspite* wouldn't steer. Worse, however, became obvious as he told Captain Packer, 'Till we get her started up again, all our armaments are temporarily out of action.'

'Blast and damn!' Packer cursed, unable to contain his anger. 'No guns in the middle of all this.' He indicated the smoke-shrouded beachhead. 'Once the Hun gets on to it, he'll be after us with every damned plane he's got!' He shook his head fiercely like a boxer attempting to shake off a bad uppercut and regained control of himself. He turned to his signals officer: 'All right, let GHQ have this: Situation unattractive . . . ship heavily damaged . . . can't steam . . . shipped five thousand tons of seawater . . . draught increased by about five feet . . .' It was hammerblow after blow, which sounded to the young signals officer, a blood-stained bandage wrapped hurriedly round his wounded forehead, like nails being driven one by one into the poor old *Warspite*'s coffin.

For Petty Officer Jim Hawkins, what had happened after the first flying bomb had struck home had been all hearsay. He remembered lying only on the debris-littered deck, his trousers for some reason filled with sticky warm liquid, at peace with himself, not even feeling any pain, staring numbly at the headless corpse opposite. The sight neither repelled him nor made him feel he had to get up and do something. Indeed, all he felt was a certain detached curiosity. Idly, he wondered why the body was without a head – he couldn't think of any particular reason why it should be – and who it belonged to.

It was only after the aid party came blundering up through the smoke, fighting their way through the jumble of twisted, tortured girders and stanchions, with someone crying, 'Over here, sir . . . There's another one, here Surgeon Commander!' that he was able to recognize the body. It was that of Hairless Harry. Later he reasoned he had smiled at the thought that his old 'oppo' would never have to worry about his lack of hair again. Then the stretcher party had picked him up, a wave of red-hot electric pain had shot through his body, the Surgeon Commander

153

had pressed a needle into his upper arm and he had slipped away into blessed oblivion . . .

Now, four months later, Jim Hawkins knew he'd never serve on the *Warspite* again. From what he had heard on the grapevine, after Old ABC had visited the gravely damaged ship at Gib, and insisted she should be repaired and readied for the final battle in Europe – they said he'd had tears in his eyes when he had seen the state of the Old Lady – she was back where she had started: with the 5th Battle Squadron in Scapa Flow from where she had fought in the Great War.

But she was no longer her old self and Hawkins, living for the buzzes on her progress, heard that one boiler room would never be drained, one turret was permanently out of action and she would never make more than twenty knots at the most. Still, it was stated that Old ABC was determined she'd take part in the D-Day landings and had packed her with 'HO Men', many of the younger ones never having been to sea before. But they were young and fit and probably enthusiastic with illusions. 'Not a bloody old crock like yours truly with one leg shorter than the other,' as he had explained ruefully to his new oppo, the Yank, 'and a ruddy silver plate in the back of his nut.'

Still, Jim Hawkins was not so disillusioned that he wanted no more of the war. Just like his old ship, on which he would now never serve again before they sent her off to the knackers' yard, which they would undoubtedly do after D-Day, he wanted to be in at the final victory. He told himself he and a lot of good mates had shed their blood for it; it was his duty and his right to be there when they finally beat the Jerries.

Now, as he waited with the rest of the assembled petty officers, he wondered what their findings would be. Would he be fit enough with his gammy leg and battered old head to train to run a landing barge? He'd had very little actual nautical training. All the same, he reasoned, he could handle the controls of a landing barge easily enough – if they took him.

In the event, Jim Hawkins need not have worried. For he and the rest were not fated to meet the medical clearing board. Instead, the old CPO with the bulbous red drinker's nose ushered them into a side room, with a knowing wink and then whispered, 'All hush-hush, lads. But one thing I can tell yer, yer'll be keeping them nice crowns and stripes, me hearties.'

Al Gore looked puzzled at Jim. 'And what's that supposed to mean? I swear you limeys speak a different lingo from us Americans.'

But before Hawkins could comment on the statement, a strange figure strode into the side room and the CPO, springing to attention, saluting at the same time, cried in his parade-ground voice, 'Officer on parade! Stand to attention!'

Awkwardly the petty officers of the various Allied nations did so. The officer didn't seem to notice their lack of military respect. Instead, he touched his one hand to his tarnished battered old white cap and said jauntily, 'All right, chaps, park it again.'

Al Gore grinned and said out of the wide of his mouth, 'I like that – park it.' Dutifully they did so, and for a moment Jim Hawkins had time to study the naval officer of a type he'd never seen before.

For a start, he was dressed in army battledress, dyed navy blue, though he wore a Royal Navy cap and WWI-style naval jackboots of a kind that had long gone out of fashion. But it was his poor battered face and arm that really attracted the young petty officer's interest.

Over his left eye he bore a black patch, which indicated that his eye was gone. There was a livid scar running down

155

the other side of his face from temple to jaw and his left hand was missing. In its place, a bright shining steel hook peeped from beneath the sleeve of his battledress blouse, complete with a cork from a bottle of wine covering the hook's point!

But despite the young officer's manifold injuries, he seemed cheerful enough. Glancing around his audience with a merry glint in his one eye, he stated, 'When I deserted the Free State Navy to help the English win the war, I was 'handsome' O'Flynn. Indeed, there was some talk that I looked somewhat like old Errol.' – He meant Errol Flynn, the swashbuckling actor. – 'Since that day, Old Jerry has rearranged my appearance a little and I feel that I look more like Horatio, my first name, today.' He grinned, showing a mouthful of excellent teeth. 'Horatio Nelson to be exact.'

His audience grinned. Lt. Commander Horatio O'Flynn was obviously a bit of a card and very definitely different from your typical lieutenant commander. Not many of them would have admitted deserting the Republic of Ireland's navy to join the Royal, though many Irish sailors and soldiers had done so since 1939; the Irish had always loved a fight, regardless of the cause or country they fought for.

'Now, gentlemen,' the officer continued, 'I'll make it short and sweet and then you can be off, making life dangerous for the virgins – if there are any left – of this parish. I'm offering you the chance to join Combined Ops.' He indicated the red and blue anchor and tommy-gun badge of Combined Operations on his shoulder. 'There'll be no extra pay for getting yourselves killed quicker than normal. But I can assure you all that you'll be contributing more to the war than on those big floating battlewagons that you've been accustomed to.' Again he grinned, but there was no answering light in his blue eye; he was too busy sizing them up, Hawkins could see that. Rapidly he began to like Lt. Commander Horatio O'Flynn.

'Your job will be simple. You'll be taking in the invading troops, our own and the Yanks and any other silly bugger who decides to go along and get the chop – more than likely – on the beaches. I'm not gonna go down on my knees to ask you to volunteer for Combined Ops. All I can say, the more of you who do, the more likely we'll get this bloody business over with. And I tell ye this, boyos,' he added hastily, 'we might be training in some godforsaken places like Slapton Sands and the like, but the unit will be based right here in Pompey. Now what do you say to that as an offer? The sooner we get this over, the sooner we'll be out of here and rid of the sawbones and tucking into several kegs of ale that I've ordered out of my own pocket for your lordships . . . !'

Jim Hawkins looked at Al Gore.

The American returned his smile. 'He's crazy,' he said. 'He's gonna get us killed. But he's just made us an offer that a thirsty gob simply can't refuse. 'He rose to his feet and said loudly, 'Commander, where do I sign up, sir?'

Two

B y May, the assorted group of petty officers who had
been 'beached', were settling down to this new and
strenuous life in Combined Operations. Technically, Jim
Hawkins and his comrades didn't find handling the clumsy
barges too difficult. It was the weather and the troops which
caused them problems. As Hawkins told Al Gore after yet
another day of 'hitting the beach' at Slapton Sands, 'Al,
I never realized the human gut could contain that much
spew. I've got a bunch of KP men cleaning the craft out
with hosepipes and I reckon they won't be finished before
lights out.'

Al Gore nodded his agreement: 'The swell makes real
horses' asses of 'em, I know. I swear I saw a seasick GI
crap into his helmet the other day.'

But, despite the rough seas and the effect they had on
the sensitive stomachs of the GIs preparing for the great
cross-Channel assault, the petty officers liked the life.
For suddenly they discovered they were their own masters,
miniature skippers, with no senior officers harassing them
all the time (though Horatio O'Flynn could be very sharp-
tongued, in his Irish way, when he wanted). It was entirely
their responsibility to get the unwieldly, box-like craft to
the shoreline, bring down the ramp and discharge the GIs
into the shallow water (already they had several cases of
heavily laden soldiers going straight to the bottom of the
sea in deep water, drowned without a chance by the weight
of their equipment).

Time and time again, day after weary, wet day, they ran through the same outline: the training convoy offshore; headquarters ships buzzing with signals; dispatch riders and drivers of halftracks, revving their engines like highly strung thoroughbreds at the starting gate, impatient to be off; tank drivers openly praying that their amphibious equipment would work so that they'd not go plunging to the bottom of the Channel – and naturally the usual GIs being sick into their helmet-liners, as they lined up in their serials with their numbers chalked on their helmets.

Flares, whistles, angry hoarse cries from officers and noncoms, tannoy voices, metallic and distorted, crying, 'Now hear this . . . now all troops hear this!' And then it would start yet once again. The rattle of rusty anchor chains. The burst of the ear-splitting noise of the engines being started up everywhere, and suddenly, startlingly, a furious hellish racket as flight after flight of scarlet rockets from barge-borne mattress batteries saturated the beach. They were followed by the Spitfires and the Mustangs winging in at zero feet, churning the water below into a crazy, white fury. Like frightened tortoises, the GIs in their barges ducked their heads, their churning stomachs forgotten for a brief moment, and then they'd be fighting the swell, the ugly box-like craft stubbornly refusing to keep their ramps to the beach.

Yet although it had become routine by now, Hawkins and the rest were still aware of the deadly seriousness of their task. If they didn't hit the beach square on or dump the craft on some sand spit, their passengers would be sitting ducks, easy targets for the dug-in Germans they'd soon be meeting on the other side of the Channel, mercilessly slaughtered before they had time to fire as much as one round from their rifles.

O'Flynn was aware of it, too. Careless and flamboyant as he was in the grand, bold Irish manner, he could be a strict taskmaster on the beach, shouting angry instructions from his megaphone, chewing out both petty officers and officers, more than once drawing his .38 with his one good hand and threatening to shoot some defaulter 'here and bloody now, if you pull a damnfool trick like that again, d'yer hear me!' But in the evening, enjoying what he called his 'ball o'malt', he'd be his calm friendly self once more, mixing easily with both the non-commissioned officers and commissioned ones, praising their efforts of the day, and always adding that final phrase of his, as if it were part of some religious creed, 'Remember, boyos, it's their lives you've got in yer hands.' And all of them, even the dullest, knew whose lives he meant.

Still, on the evenings in the crowded hard-drinking pubs in Pompey, Jim Hawkins' heart would miss a beat when he recognized a matelot from the fleet and he'd move over, even 'putting out the boat' now and again for a free pint, to pump the sailor or petty officer for news of the old *Warspite*.

There was not much to find out. The new crew of the *Warspite* was what the Royal Navy called 'a passenger crew', one that had brought her home after preliminary repairs to extensive damage at Gib. They had been forced to stay on, a makeshift bunch, who were finding it hard to create some sort of cohesion. Still, according to his various informants, the Old Lady and her matelots were doing their best, though invariably the sailor, finishing his free pint of 'wallop', would comment before departing into the blacked-out gloom outside in the bombed streets, 'She ain't what she used to be, the old *Warspite*, shipmate. She won't last much longer. Ta for the pig's ear. Ta-ta for now . . .'

And the news that the Old Lady wasn't what she had once been when he had first joined as an eager young seaman back in '39 in what now seemed a different age, disheartened him temporarily. It made him feel old somehow, as if his time had run its course and that he, too, was as knackered as the *Warspite* and that it was time for him 'to pack it all in', as a hard little voice at the back of his mind phrased it (though he never liked to interpret what it meant by 'packing it in'). Then, in common with many of his fellow petty officers, he'd go on the razzle, drinking his pay away until he'd stagger into the streets, weave his way back to his billet and fall into a deep sleep, from which he'd awake with an aching head and a numbness that would carry him through till the next time.

There were the women of course. As Al Gore phrased it, 'All ya need, Jim, old buddy, is a bit of the old 4 Fs. Find 'em, feel 'em, fuck 'em and forget 'em. You take it from somebody who knows, that's the best way a gob can take his mind off what's to come . . . and what's to come don't bear thinking about.' And his new-found friend was right until what happened that day on the beach at Slapton Sands.

It was one of those unnecessary accidents that happen at war. There are enough determined troops on both sides ready to kill the enemy at the drop of a hat. It is something to be expected and, in a way, justified. But an act of carelessness resulting, in what the brass called friendly fire – 'Yeah, friendly fire that kills ya fucking dead,' the GIs would crack bitterly – that was hard to take.

Thus it was that Jim Hawkins came to be taking in a barge-load of GIs on what appeared to be just another routine mission, when it happened. The landing barge was coming to Slapton Sands at a cracking pace, bow-on for a change, striking each wave with a stomach-churning thud as if the craft was hitting a series of solid brick walls. Hawkins flashed a glance behind him at the kids in their heavy helmets. They looked as if they might be on some summer-camp adventure training, chewing solidly in the fashion of GIs. He asked himself if they realized that perhaps in weeks, even days, they'd be doing this for real: that it was a deadly game from which many of them might not return. If they did, their innocent young faces revealed nothing of that knowledge. They continued to chew like cows chewing cud. He sighed and concentrated on his task, as the beach loomed up ever closer.

Gunfire was now pounding the heights above the beach, edging ever closer to the ruined Devon village, which had been evacuated by the reluctant locals that year. Naturally, the ships carrying out the bombardment were using live ammo. But that didn't worry Hawkins. Ex-naval gunner himself, he knew just how careful gunnery officers were; they'd lift or cease firing once the landed troops got too close. But Jim Hawkins had not reckoned with the amateur US gunners manning the rocket batteries, which would give close support to the assaulting infantry.

Now he was bringing the ugly awkward barge into land, as everywhere huge brown steaming holes appeared in the foreground like the work of giant moles. Smoke drifted on all sides. The air was filled with the acrid stench of burned explosive, as he cried, 'Down ramp!'

With a clatter, the front of the barge opened up. The US lieutenant leading the infantry cried, 'Follow me, guys!' And then the soldiers, bayonets flashing, were pelting through the shallows to left and right, roaring their heads off. But not for long. Suddenly there was a tremendous crash to his rear. It was the floating rocket battery. With a banshee-like howl a quiver of rockets seared up into the burning, smoke-filled sky. Next moment they were howling down again in an elemental fury. They struck the beach a tremendous blow. Hawkins gasped, as the very air was sucked from his lungs. His face was slapped by the impact like a blow from an open palm. He blinked. When he opened his eyes, the beach in front of him was a crazy panorama of flying bodies being flung on all sides in a gory mess of flailing, severed limbs.

He gasped, as if being strangled to death. He caught a frightening glimpse of a head, complete with helmet, rolling along the beach to come to stop at the edge of the water like a kid's abandoned ball. Then the fog of war descended once more and obscured that scene of mayhem and savage murder, and Jim Hawkins knew, as he vomited, that yet again one of those pointless tragedies of war had occurred . . .

It was that same night that the woman looked across at him in the snug of the pub he sometimes frequented when he wanted to be alone – and this night he very definitely wanted to be alone after the friendly fire slaughter of the morning. He knew from the way she looked at him that she knew he was drunk. Not that it worried him. This night he'd like to stand up and shout, 'To fuck with yer war . . . *FUCK IT!*' But being the man he was, he knew even in his drunken haze, that he couldn't do that.

The final toll had been thirteen killed and double that number seriously wounded, some already with their limbs amputated there and then on the beach. Christ Almighty, he muttered to himself as he ordered yet another double, looking threateningly at the man behind the bar, just challenging him to say 'We've run out of Scotch', they're dead before they've even started to live. He tossed off the Scotch, as if it were water and remembered the US naval commander in charge saying carelessly, 'Fortunes of war, petty officer . . . There'll be no inquiry. You can't make an omelette, ya know, without breaking eggs.' Of course there'd be no fucking inquiry! Someone had made an elementary maths mistake on the rocket barrage and he, the commander, was responsible in the final analysis. Naturally he wasn't going to risk his gold rings to take the can back for some thick bastard of a 'junior grade looey', as the Yanks called them.

The woman smiled at him. She wasn't particularly pretty, though she had warm good eyes. Nor did she look like a good-time girl, the sort who haunted Pompey's pubs and bars these days, especially when there were Yanks in town. God, how they loved the Yanks with their money, goodies and fifteen-denier nylons. He smiled back.

The woman took her time.

In the mirror behind the bar he saw how she uncrossed her legs. Deliberately. He caught a glimpse of plump white flesh above the black silk stockings. He felt a slight urge of sexual interest. As drunk as he was, he began to become sexually excited. Then he thought of the dead GIs sprawled out in the churned wet sand in the grotesque abandoned poses of those done violently to death and told himself he should not be interested. But the woman was.

Abruptly, giving him a long look in the mirror, she rose and came towards him. Her face was serious. There was none of the good-time girl's come-hither look. Indeed she looked *very* serious. She stopped and without preamble said, 'You don't look too happy, petty officer. I don't think drink helps much, do you?'

Her approach caught him completely off guard. He rose unsteadily. With undue formality for that kind of place, he said, 'Won't you sit down?'

'No,' she answered firmly and surprised him again. 'I only came here to meet someone like you.' Now he noticed that she was dressed in black and that she wore her wedding ring on the opposite hand. She was a recent widow. 'Do you follow me?'

'I—'

'If you want another bottle,' she interrupted him in a low but firm voice, 'slip Freddie over there an extra five bob and the price and he'll oblige. We can take it with us.'

'But where're we going?' he asked, completely confused.

'Home . . . to my house.' Her eyes remained unsmiling, but there was a sudden momentary tremor in her voice, as she added. 'Please.'

He swallowed, feeling a nerve at the side of his head begin to tick. 'I'll get a bottle . . . Stay there, while I go to . . . er . . . Freddie . . . Please don't run away.'

'I won't,' she answered solemnly.

As she waited, the black-out curtain was swept hesitantly to one side. In the mirror she saw the one-armed man framed there in his dyed dark-blue battledress, adorned by great chocolate-brown patches like those of a clown's motley.

In that same moment the man behind the bar saw the intruder, too. He frowned. She wondered why the former prisoner-of-war looked harmless. These days they were everywhere, working in the fields, clearing away the bomb rubble in Pompey, even working at the naval docks. Why, officially they were called 'co-belligerents', for although they had fought against us at the beginning of the war, they had been our allies since the previous year.

But obviously all that didn't impress the elderly barman. He raised his hand, crying, 'Get out of here, you Eyetie bastard! We ain't having no greasers in this here pub. Now sling yer bleeding hook.'

The man at the door fled.

Then the half-drunk petty officer, with the sad eyes, was back carrying Freddie's black-market bottle of cheap booze and she forgot all about the 'co-belligerent'.

'You married, Jim?' she asked. She kissed him again even before he could answer. She plumped down in the old cracked leather sofa, still clutching his black-market bottle and with her coat still on, poked the last dying embers of the pathetic fire. 'No,' he answered, as she did so. 'Never the time . . . Never the opportunity.'

Outside, the church clock chimed midnight. All was silent save the soft pace of an air-raid warden down in the ruined street. The old house echoed the chimes sadly. They might well have been the last people on earth alive. 'You?' he felt he ought to ask.

'Was,' she answered, finally getting a wavering little flame from the poor wartime coal. 'Went down in the *Barham*.'

'I remember her. Didn't have a chance.'

She made no comment, but sat down next to him, her coat still on. He put his arm around her. She was shivering. 'Do you want a drink?' he asked. 'Warm you up a bit. Freezing in here.'

'It's not the cold,' she began and then stopping, adding, 'All right. You'll find a mug and a glass in the cupboard.'

He shook his head. 'No, I think I've had enough for the time being. Later perhaps.' Suddenly the sight of all those dead GIs had flashed before his mind's eye and it had sobered him. Why should he be sitting here, half-drunk with a friendly, warm-hearted woman and the prospect of a night in bed with her. And the others were dead; the lot of them perhaps nineteen-year-old virgins? It didn't seem fair. No, that was not the right description. But for the life of him he couldn't find the right word. Instead, he turned to the waiting woman and said without preamble, 'Do you want me to stay?'

'Of course, Jim,' she answered, her face kindly, but really revealing nothing, he thought later. 'You're my Saturday night treat – remember, like when we were kids.' Abruptly she grinned, as if at some private joke. 'It goes with a bath in a tin tub in front of the fire and a change of knickers for the week.'

He grinned with her. He liked her approach. Life was

far too complicated for him to understand it any more. This was the way it should be. 'Sharp's the word, quick's the action,' as the long dead CPO Higgins used to say in another time. 'Do you often give yersen Saturday night treats?' he asked in the same bantering manner she had used.

'Not often,' she answered. 'But I wouldn't mind a drink now before we go to bed.'

'Natch,' he answered. He rose swiftly, no longer unsteady on his feet. He found the mug and the glass. He filled hers and added a little water, deciding she'd get the glass. When he turned, she had slipped out of her coat and her dress too. She had a fine womanly figure in the cheap crêpe-de-Chine petticoat. Her nipples had become erect and poked through the glistening material. It might have been the cold, but he hoped it was caused by sexual excitement.

'You're cold,' he said, handing her the glass.

'Maybe,' she answered. 'But if I am, you'll soon see I'm warm between the sheets,' she added softly and smiled up at him.

'I'll do my best.'

'Of course you will. Now, let's knock this back and get into bed. We're wasting time and time is—'

'What we ain't got lots of' He beat her to it.

Five minutes later they were locked in each other's arms, consumed by a frenzy of passion, and time was forgotten – for the while.

At about two she awoke. She turned on her back, hands beneath her head. At her side, he snored softly on the sweaty, rumpled pillow. She peered at his handsome young face in the chink of cold moonlight that came through a tear in the blackout curtain.

There was no movement in his face. None of that twitching of men when they have been excited, as he had been. The face revealed nothing. Apart from the soft snore,

Petty Officer Jim Hawkins might well have already been dead . . .

Now it was almost June. The training had ceased. There was nothing more that the soldiers could learn. Besides, as Jim Hawkins and the rest of the petty officers of Combined Operations knew, the troops had been locked under armed guard in their pre-invasion cages. Once in, they were not to be let out till the 'Day' came.

Indeed, a dull heavy mood seemed to have settled over the country. The wait had been too long. Four years for some. Besides, the raids on London and the south coast had commenced once more after months, even years, of raid-free nights. There were rumours, too, of worse to come: terrible weapons which fell silently out of the sky; perhaps even poison gas.

The weather over the south couldn't have been better, however. The countryside basked in warm sunshine. The Channel, that stretch of water they would soon cross into the unknown, was calm and glistening, even beautiful of an evening in the dying sun. Yet for the soldiers and civilians, the fine summery weather only heightened the feeling of emptiness. It had all taken too long. There had been too many years of emptiness, so many hard years of preparation. Now the test was here. Would they – could they – succeed now?

Lt. Commander Horatio O'Flynn, quiet for a change, seemed to sense the mood of the men under his command. They had still not been consigned to the cages. They had work to do on the barges; there was always something going wrong with the ugly steel boxes. So they remained in Portsmouth, but were forbidden to leave the area, if they could have dodged the MPs who were everywhere.

Whenever he had the opportunity and there were enough of his men present, he lectured them in his roundabout, unpedantic Irish way. No mention of the great cause. Not a single eternal verity of the kind loved by the politicians. No hate. No question of revenge on the Nazis. Just duty, courage and confidence. 'We get them across, lads. We land 'em,' he would say, a wry smile on his Irish face, 'and then we scuttle off back home to safety and live to tell the tale to our grandkids, if they'll believe the bugger, and die tucked up in a nice warm bed.' Then he'd add invariably, 'In the meantime, me boyos, if I was in your shoes and not an officer and an Irish gentlemen, as you well know, I'd get myself a nice ball o'malt and a plump pigeon o' a woman to keep me warm in bed before . . .' And there he would end, leaving his sentence unfinished. But they all knew what he meant and those who could took his advice, including Al Gore.

For Al, it seemed to Hawkins, was not convinced that he'd live to tell the tale to his grandkids. 'Ner,' he'd maintain, 'Mrs Gore's handsome son ain't going home to the land of the round doorknob no more, Jim. So what d'ya say – we'd rather fuck than fight!' And off he'd go, with whatever rations he could steal or barter from the cooks in the petty officers' mess to pay for his latest 'piece of tail'. And Hawkins would watch him go, telling himself, that perhaps O'Flynn was wrong and that cynical realist Al Gore was right. But if Gore bought it, did that mean that the others would get the chop, too? It was a thought that he didn't dare take to its logical conclusion.

And in the blacked-out streets of Pompey, the Mad Italian wandered, dodging the police patrols, looting the abandoned houses, stealing from unattended American jeeps, living from hand to mouth, talking, talking, talking all the time in that crazy doomed fashion of his – and looking.

'But what am I looking for?' he would stop abruptly from time and time and shoot the question at himself.

There would be no answer, only the sound of the wind over that dividing sea and the steady drone of the unseen planes overhead on guard in the darkness.

Then he would go on again, muttering that demented litany of his until the heavy footfall would indicate the approach of a special constable or an MP patrol and he would scurry, hunch-backed, to hide in the ruins like some human rat.

Three

The squally rain had ceased. Now the great battleship plodded on steadily, her new paint still gleaming in the raindrops. In the immediate area, the little fleet she commanded did the same. It could have been a peacetime squadron out on a training exercise, save for the presence of the ugly monitor, armed with monstrous 15-inch guns, her decks almost level with the grey-green water.

But the crew now assembling on the quarterdeck to hear Captain Kelsey's address had no eyes for the odd mix of cruisers, battleships, gunboats and the like which made up HMS *Warspite*'s assault squadron. Instead, their gaze was fixed on their new skipper, for even the dullest of the crew knew he would not have had the whole of the ship's crew assembled if he didn't want to tell them something of vital importance. And after tossing in the early June gales for nearly three days, they had realized they were not out here in the dangerous Channel for the fun of it. This was the invasion, they were sure of that.

Kelsey, like all new captains who hadn't got the feel of his mixed crew yet, didn't waste time on small talk. He got down to business at once. Using the newfangled mike, instead of the old-fashioned loud-hailer, he ordered the thousand-odd officers and men to stand at ease and then launched into his reason for assembling them this Sunday morning. 'We are now officially "Force D",' he announced. 'So you know what that means – the invasion.'

173

Kelsey didn't give the crew time to indulge in the usual murmurs and subdued comments which normally resulted from important news. 'It's going to be our job to add heavy firepower to the assault of the British and Canadian forces on three beaches running from east to west code-named "Sword", "Juno" and "Gold". Don't ask me about the names. I don't know why they've given them such idiotic names.' It was his one attempt to make a personal comment, even a mild joke. It didn't work. The crew were too eager to hear what he had to say next. 'We are therefore what is called the Eastern Task Force. Now, the Americans will be landing at two beaches code-named "Utah" and "Omaha". There the Americans will receive extra firepower from three of their own battleships and several cruisers. This force will be named – naturally – the Western Task Force. However, their Lordships think that the Yanks might run into trouble on their beaches—'

'As usual,' someone commented ironically from the lower deck. Almost immediately the nearest petty officers started whipping out their notebooks to note the name of the culprit who had dared to interrupt the captain. Someone would be on the 'rattle' before the parade was over.

'So it has been decided in that eventuality, the *Warspite* will switch from the Eastern Task Force to aid the western one. It has all been worked out and we shall be preceded by as many as forty minesweepers to sweep new channels through any Hun minefields.'

That impressed even the cynical 'old heads' of the lower deck. Forty mine-sweepers to protect one single squadron was a tremendous number of ships. Even at Dunkirk there had never been that number of minesweepers.

'As for air cover,' Kelsey went on, 'just look at the sky. There are our planes everywhere. This time, for those of you who were on the Old Lady at Salerno, not a single

Hun plane will get within sniffing distance of her skirts, I can assure you.'

This time the new skipper gave a pause and allowed his crew to smile. Then his face hardened again and he continued, 'I don't have to tell you men the state the *Warspite* is in. She has come to about the end of the line. My personal guess is that this will be her last major action of World War Two before she is decommissioned and scrapped. Let us ensure she doesn't fail and that she goes out in a blaze of glory.' He stepped back, the microphone went dead and it was all over. Solemnly the crew broke from the divisions and went to their various duty stations. Unusually there was little chat. Even the petty officers seemed to refrain from their usual harassment and banter; the mood of the sailors was too sober.

Two hours later they were out in the open Channel. A few of the matelots stood listlessly at the rails, watching the Needles drop behind gradually before vanishing into the growing dusk. The mood was flat and grey. Indeed, to the sailors everything appeared grey: the bleak sea, the sullen evening sky, life itself.

Now there was no shore remaining to be seen. A wall of dusk was creeping in from the sea. No sound was apparent either, save that of the ship's turbines and the muted drone of their aerial escort hidden in the clouds. Then they were gone, vanished into the darkness. HMS *Warspite*, the seventh and last of her line in nearly three centuries of British sea warfare was sailing to her last battle . . .

'Information has just been received,' the metallic voice announced over the tannoy system, 'about a new Hun mine. As yet it has no official designation. Our American allies call it a "Bouncing Betty".'

The reference to the American allies roused a hollow weary laugh from the still sea-sick GIs who had been on the stinking, fetid landing barge for nearly forty-eight hours now. 'Our chaps in the Eighth Army call it the 50-50 mine. You might ask why. The reason, according to the London Ministry of War, is that the mine contains sharp steel rods. The name derives from the unfortunate soldier's chances if he steps on one. If he hits it with the right foot, the rods fly up, past his right side. If he hits it with his left, on the other hand, he'll be a singing tenor for the rest of his life.'

Jim Hawkins might have laughed at the comedian on the tannoy, but the look on the faces of the GIs told him it would be wiser not to.

He looked at the green-glowing dial of his watch yet again. Soon they would be off, Hawkins was sure of that. The GIs had had time now to recover from their ordeal of these last gale-rent thirty-six hours. It appeared to him that there was a window in the weather at this moment. If they didn't take it, God knows how long they would have to wait for a second chance and knowing the Yanks as he knew them now, they wouldn't stand for another twenty-four hours on the barge. They'd mutiny!

But where was Al? As soon as they had returned, battered, bruised and miserable to the rendezvous point off Weymouth, he had been summoned urgently to the port to meet O'Flynn. Why, Hawkins didn't know. He did know, however, that the one-armed Irishman was keeping his buddy, as he now called Gore in the American fashion, a hell of a long time. What was so important that they needed a run-of-the mill US petty officer at Naval HQ?

Hawkins dismissed his friend. He'd be there when needed, that was for sure. For all his cynicism, Gore would be eager to be in at the kill; all the old-timers were. They'd waited years for this opportunity. Come what may they weren't going to miss it . . .

O'Flynn had had a few of his 'balls o' malt', as he called

them, Al Gore could see that. After all it took a lush to see a lush, and O'Flynn, despite the hour, was well and truly pickled. Still, as Gore had always asserted, 'Rank hath its privileges' and officers could do 'just what the Sam Hill they liked'. So he waited till the Irishman finished the last of his Scotch and told him why he had been summoned here at this time of the day.

Outside, now the blackout had been lifted, he could see the packed harbour, with so many small ships and craft lined up that he thought you might be able to walk from ship to ship right across Weymouth Bay. And everywhere there were GIs eating, sleeping, playing cards – at six in the morning – in card games that appeared to have been going on for weeks. There was even one guy, he could just see, having a butterfly with an old whore in a secluded doorway. She had her skirt up and he had his slacks down about his ankles, humping her like a fiddler's elbow. For a moment he envied the kid, although the whore with her raddled contorted, powdered face was twice his age. At least *he* was doing something constructive.

'O'Flynn followed the direction of his gaze and said, 'So this is the story, Gore. I'm asking you first, however, to volunteer before I go into details.' He grinned. 'Now that's a silly Mick's way of putting it, isn't it just?'

Gore didn't rise to the bait. Instead he said, 'Volunteer for what?'

'Something bloody dangerous, Gore. But then this day and tomorrow there won't be anything that isn't dangerous, will there? Even that bold young sapleen out there might get a dose o' clap before the day's out, eh?'

Gore relaxed. 'Gimme a slug of that Scotch, sir,' he snorted, his mind made up already, 'and I'll volunteer to go to hell and back.'

'Spoken like a brave fellah indeed.' O'Flynn pushed over

what was left in the bottle. 'There you are. Help yerself – and bad cess on your enemies.'

Gore didn't bother to ask for a glass. Instead he took a mighty slug from the bottle neck, gasped with the shock of the powerful drink and, wiping the back of his hand across his wet lips, said, 'I've just volunteered, sir.'

'Good,' O'Flynn said and now his smile vanished. 'All right, this is the drill. To cover the landings, there'll be five capital ships, all armed with 15-inch guns, three from your Yank navy and two from ours. Now the Jerries have nothing on land to tackle guns of that size. As long as the battleships keep bombarding the Huns' forward artillery positions our boys will be safe. You understand?'

'Yessir,' Gore answered dutifully, though in reality he didn't. What had the battlewagons of the fleet got to do with him volunteering?

'Now,' O'Flynn told him, 'as far as I have been told, each capital ship will carry some 150 rounds of 15-inch high explosive and about twenty fewer rounds of armour-piercing. Each time the individual ship fires a volley, that's fifteen shells or in some cases nine. So if she fires over a period of a couple of hours she'll soon be out of ammo for her main armament.'

Gore nodded his understanding.

'And that means she has to return to Portsmouth to replenish. In that period she is not covering the beaches and, knowing the Huns, they could be up to all sorts of fiendish Hun tricks in the meantime.' O'Flynn tried his Irish humour, but it didn't work. His one eye remained too serious, too worried.

'So instead of the battlewagons returning to port to replenish,' Gore beat him to it, 'we take the ammo to the battlewagons.'

'Clever people the Yanks,' O'Flynn said. 'Exactly. We want you and a few other experienced petty officers we have picked to reload immediately. You won't be taking the footsloggers across, you'll be taking 15-inch shells instead, Gore.'

The American gave him a weak smile. 'At least shells don't puke all over the damned craft.'

O'Flynn didn't respond. The matter was too serious. 'You know, of course, what a near miss'll do?'

Gore finished the rest of the Scotch and gasped, 'Well, my old pop allus said, I'd make a handsome corpse – *the bastard*!'

The woman nodded. In the corner, pretending to wield a brush, muttering to himself as always, the Mad Italian caught the look. He turned and grunted, as if he were finding it particularly difficult to clean the corner and, still bent double, eyed the US petty officer in his British battledress. He swayed slightly as he passed as if he hadn't a care in the world; the Italian could smell the drink on his breath. In his crazy fashion, he told himself that the *Americano* was going to be easy meat. He finished his job, used his one arm to place the broom over his right shoulder and marched off, as if he were aping the two Marine sentries at the gate of naval HQ. They were not offended. The one chuckled and said, 'Doolally tap, Charley.'

'Ner,' the other responded. 'Too much pulling their plonkers.' He made an explicit obscene gesture with his free hand. 'All them Eyetie POWs are at it like frigging fiddlers' elbows. Sex-starved they are.'

'That's not what I hear,' his mate hinted darkly and then quickly. 'Officer coming. His nibs – the pride of the Irish.' He snapped to attemtion, the crazy POW forgotten already . . .

Mae had spotted him a month before. She had naturally

heard of him by then. He was well known in the central area around the bombed Portsmouth Guildhall. They said he was on release from some Italian POW camp or other; there were a lot of them like that, billeted on farmers, small factory owners and the like, free to come and go for the most part. Besides, strong young men, both Italian and German, were at a premium, and not too many questions were asked about them. Though she had thought the first time she had had a good look at Adolfo (that name usually caused some ribald comment) that he did look more German, with his long fresh-coloured face and blond hair, than the other Italians she had met since they had become 'co-belligerents' and could move about so freely.

At first she had just taken pity on him – the missing arm and his occasional outburst of crazy talk in a language she couldn't understand anyway. She'd fed him a couple of times and he had provided the food, watching *her* as they ate, as if she were the one who needed feeding up. Indeed, thereafter he had started bringing her food, once a couple of chickens he must have stolen somewhere or other, urging her in his accented English, 'You eat . . . good for body . . . come, missus, you eat.'

But it had not stopped at food and friendship. For the first time in her life she started to realize that she lusted after him. There was no other word than lust, though it wasn't one she had ever dreamed of using. It had not been a word found normally in the vocabulary of a woman of her type. At times she simply could not keep her eyes off his loins, the way his trousers bulged there or when he sat down and his penis slipped to the side of his trousers and hung there, along the upper length of his thigh, so temptingly that she had forcibly to restrain herself from reaching out trembling fingers to touch it.

The evening he brought her some bottles of – probably stolen – beer and urged her to drink with his usual broken

'Drink, missus . . . good,' she was not able to stop herself. He had sipped a bottle of warm ale and then, putting it down, obviously feeling it wasn't to his taste, had fallen into a deep sleep on her battered horsehair couch – even the papers with which she had stuffed its innards had not hindered his sleep. Again, that tempting length of flesh had slipped to the side of his pants, as he lay there, breathing hard, legs spread, and this time the combination of his defencelessness and the ale had killed all her inhibitions. She had reached out and as gently as she could, afraid to wake him, her heart beating frantically like a trip-hammer with excitement, she had touched it. Even through the thick serge it had seemed burningly hot to her. Once started, she had been unable to stop herself. She had begun to work it up and down in a manner that she had never done for any other man in her life. For even in her drunkenness and passion, she wanted to give *him* pleasure. She had to. Indeed, she had never experienced such a desire: an ecstasy of devotion and sexual excitement that made her feel wet between the legs and shake as if she were afflicted by some terrible fever.

The inevitable had happened. They had become lovers; lovers of the strangest kind, hardly able to communicate with each other, save in bed, where Adolfo, insatiable and totally unlike any other man she had known sexually, thrilled her in ways she couldn't have believed possible. For his was a silent love. No silly words were wasted. No daft jokes. None of the usual props of sexual excitement – the black stockings, the lingerie, the garter belt. His kind of love was totally animal, passionate, savage, inhuman so that at times her ecstasy fringed on fear. But fear or not, she couldn't stop. She had to continue. There was no alternative. Why, she started to shake with excitement as soon as he came through the door, tall, blond, muttering to himself, his steel-blue eyes viewing a horizon known only to him. Then she could hardly thank him for the stolen delicacies that he always brought her before tugging him to the tiny bedroom for the one thing that now dominated her whole existence. At times she could hardly resist the overwhelming urge to start ripping at his uniform as he came through the door.

Thus it was that she didn't hesitate one second when he ordered her to go out with sailors she might be able to pick up in the pubs and bars and the illegal drinking dens of the naval port. Mae wasn't a stupid woman. She knew she was doing wrong. At the back of her mind, a little voice warned, 'He's a spy or something like that, Mae . . . you're going to get ourself in trouble if you don't watch out.'

But she hadn't heeded the warning and now she knew it was too late. The handsome young petty officer she had slept with, who had known her dead husband's ship, Adolfo had rejected for reasons known only to himself. But when she had 'entertained' the American (as she called it to herself) at his command, he had approved. The Yank had been too drunk to know whether he was coming or going in the end, and that dawn, after he had staggered off to report for duty, Adolfo had said in that funny broken English of his. '*Si, si*, he good . . . Look no more.'

Now this June morning, as the unsuspecting Yank had hurried off to commence the loading of the 15-inch shells on to his barge, as ordered by O'Flynn, she watched Adolfo, with his broom over his shoulder, follow him and knew instinctively that she needed to 'look no more', as he had ordered. The sailors she had picked and the Italian were going out of her life. She was sure of that. She paused in a doorway, the stonework pocked by the bombs of 1941 still. She felt faint for a minute and supported herself to prevent herself from falling. They were all going now. Her life was changing. With luck she'd never be found out and would live to be an old lady, who would take her secrets with her to the grave. Now she was fated to become a tiny footnote in the secret history of World War Two.

Like beasts of burden, laden with eighty pounds of equipment, each soldier's helmet marked with a chalked number, they filed up the centuries-old steps back on to the jetty. They were happy, making wisecracks at the other GIs of the 4th US Infantry Division still imprisoned in the steel shells of the stinking barges.

Gore stroked his unshaven chin. Poor assholes, he told himself, they thought they were gonna get away with it. Dopes that they were, they didn't realize that there was no turning back now. They needed bodies, a lot of bodies, on the other side. They'd be relocated. He sighed and remembered the naked body of the Englishwoman for a moment.

Four

'And the condemned man ate a hearty breakfast,' the matelot gasped as the great ship came sailing out of the smokescreen and the whole dreadful panorama of the invasion beach was revealed to the crew of the *Warspite*. A few of the Old Lady's passenger crew had been at Salerno the year before, but the D-Day beaches bore no comparison. Here, the whole might of the Free World had been seemingly assembled to blast the German defenders off the face of Europe. There were ships everywhere. They ranged from the steel boxes of invasion troop-carrying barges to the mighty battlewagons of the fleets, both British and US.

On all sides there was controlled confusion. Ships raced back and forth. Troops waded up to their necks through the water heading for the mire-strewn strands, with fighters zooming in at zero feet, their cannon and machine guns chattering frantically, firing a lethal morse of shell and bullet. Cannon pounded the beaches further back, flinging huge whirling columns of shingle and sand into the air. It seemed impossible for the German defenders to survive such a cruel volume of Allied fire.

But they did. Here and there on the ridge which bordered the beach, there were the spurts of cherry-red flame and sudden puffs of dark smoke, followed moments later by the screech of a heavy shell. Out in the harbour area huge spouts of crazy-white water rushed into the dawn sky. They were followed by the zip of tracer scything the first troops still struggling through the water, ripping them apart, staining the sea dark red with their spilled blood.

Captain Kelsey, viewing that scene of destruction and sudden death through his high-powered binoculars, took it all in, in a flash. He knew that, outnumbered as they were, the Germans still had the upper hand. After all, they were fighting from long-prepared dug-in positions. Once they had pinned the assault infantry down, their sergeants and officers, the leaders, killed or dying, it would be damnably hard to get them moving again. The time for action was now, while the infantrymen were still on their feet and moving.

Action was needed immediately from the *Warspite* and those formidable guns and Kelsey was prepared to take virtually any risk to ensure that the Old Lady played her role in making a success of this great venture on which the future of the world depended. He grabbed for the blower. Without formality, he snapped, 'Guns!'

'Sir?'

'Scrap all fire-plans. No time for that. Tackle any target of opportunity that you think is dangerous. Got it – you're on your own, Guns . . . Targets of opportunity.'

'Yessir,' Guns roared back and there was no mistaking the delight in his voice. Now he could use all his specialist knowledge, without constraint from above, to employ the *Warspite* as he thought fit. It was an artillery officer's dream and he was not slow in realizing it.

Now within seconds, firing blind, without the benefit of an air or a forward observer spotting from the beach, the first huge shells, each weighing well over a hundred pounds, screeched over the heads of the hard-pressed infantry, whose dead bodies now were starting to litter that terrible beach like a khaki-coloured rug. Time and time again, they hit home. Enemy guns exploded with a massive roar. Tanks

186

hiding behind the ridge line went up in oil-tinged, flaming fury. Flak guns, batteries of them, were smashed, their gun barrels twisting and warping into grotesque, impossible shapes; as salvoes of armour-piercing shells slammed into them, best-quality Krupp steel were turned as soft as that of kids' toys by that awesome frightening impact.

Sailing back and forth at a steady ten knots, the Old Lady fought her last battle, as if she were some filly, frisky and headstrong, without a care in the world, imperiously disdaining the splashes of the German counter-fire erupting all about her. As Kelsey on his bridge, his battle pennants flying boldly above him cried, 'If the Old Lady's going to go down, then damn me, she's going to do so fighting!'

The collection of barges carrying the second wave of the 4th US Infantry Division's assault chugged slowly towards the smoke-shrouded beach. Fire from the enemy positions was desultory. The reason was discovered later. The barge force was several miles off course; they were landing on a beach, which, unknown to the planners, was barely defended. Of all the five and a half Allied divisions which would be landed this Tuesday, the 4th would come off best. Their casualties wouldn't number more than a hundred-odd.

Still, as Hawkins at the wheel of his own barge watched the first wave splashing ashore, with behind them the tank-landing ships plunging and wallowing like clumsy whales as they waited their turn to unload, he knew he couldn't afford to relax. The lives of his couple of dozen young Yanks depended upon his expertise. Salerno had taught him never to underestimate old Jerry, especially when he seemed to have his back to the wall as was the case here.

Time and time again, he started and waited as enemy star shells exploded to the right of the assault force, bathing the little boats advancing at less than five knots in their glowing silver unreal light. For he half-expected the enemy guns to be switched to this sector and then he guessed all hell would be let loose. After all, they were sitting ducks at the speed they were sailing. But nothing happened. The training exercises at Slapton Sands the previous spring had been worse than this and had caused more casualties. He sniffed and continued his present course. Five more minutes and he would be unloading his green-faced weary Yanks and returning to England – and that would be his part in Tuesday, June 6, 1944. He grinned to himself. It looked now as if he would survive after all and live to tell his grandkids about D-Day. His grin vanished as soon as it had come. But what the hell would he tell them? That he'd been a sort of glorified bus conductor, taking a bunch of scared American kids to paddle ashore on some unknown Froggie beach like a school party on the annual bank holiday outing.

Suddenly, startlingly, the roar of high-speed engines going all out cut into his reverie. He was alert immediately. He flung a glance to his left. Even as he did, the angry white tracer came racing towards the almost stationary landing craft like glowing golfballs. Next instant there was a patter of bullets off the steel side. It was like heavy tropical rain on a tin roof.

'Holy Christ!' he exclaimed as the German E-boat raced in to the convoy at a tremendous rate, its sharp bow high out of the water, the quick-firer blasting tracer shells at the unarmed barges in white fury.

Hawkins acted instinctively. He opened up the engines. All around, the other petty officer skippers reacted in their own individual fashion. Some tried to escape. Others decided to race for the beach while there was still time. But time had virtually run out. For now the bold lone E-boat skipper was among the scattering barges. As he flashed by in a huge comb of flying seawater, Hawkins caught a glimpse of him at the bridge, white cap stuck at the back of his blond head, silk scarf flying in the wind. But only a glimpse. For in that same instant a burst of tracer raked the side of the barge viciously. Hawkins ducked frantically.

A GI was too slow. Like some damned tourist rubberneck, he had stood up to watch the E-boat approach. Now he paid for his foolishness. The burst struck him straight in the face. It looked as if someone had thrown a handful of strawberry jam at his features. He went down gurgling and drowning in his own blood. Next moment the E-boat had flashed by, its quick-firer slamming tracer shells into the next barge, riddling it in a flash, tearing chunks of steel from her hull as the terrified GIs went tumbling over the side only to be borne to the bottom of the sea under the weight of their equipment.

'Fuck this for a game of soldiers,' Hawkins cried in anger and despair. He made another decision. For the moment, the marauding E-boat was occupied elsewhere; the blond skipper was having a field day. He was firing to both sides like some Hollywood cowboy on a six-shooter rampage in a frontier township. But Hawkins knew that soon the skipper would turn and race for the safety of the open sea, repeating the performance on the way back – and Hawkins didn't want to be there when he did.

'Keep your frigging heads down,' he yelled above the racket, as the first of the Spitfires fell out of the sky at a tremendous speed to begin its attack on the E-boat. 'Keep behind the steel plating, you men.'

The GIs needed no urging. They had seen what had happened to their comrade, who lay dying in a puddle of his own steaming blood in the well of the craft, where his eyes had been, now two suppurating scarlet pits.

Hastily, Hawkins swung the tiller round. Overhead the Spitfire flashed by, dragging a huge black shadow behind

it. Some of the GIs cheered. Hawkins had no time for
such nonsense. Now he was intent solely on saving his
men. The invasion could go ahead without this handful of
young soldiers. He upped the speed. Slowly, but definitely,
the battered landing barge began to disappear into the
fog of war.

'I've got spurs that jingle-jangle-jingle as I go riding
merrily along,' Petty Officer Al Gore sang happily to
himself as the heavily laden barge chugged stolidly towards
the faint smoky smudge which was the invasion beach. His
speed was a mere five knots, for he knew he'd have to wait
off-shore – '*safely* off-shore' O'Flynn had emphasized just
before he had sailed – till the tender from one of the
battlewagons picked up his cargo of fifteen-inch shells.
That would be the tricky bit, he told himself. They'd
both be stationary for the time it took his makeshift
crew of 'dinges' and a handful of Eyetie volunteers
to off-load their dangerous cargo. But by the frightened
look on their dark faces as they squatted in the supposed
cover of the shell-cases, Gore didn't think it'd take them
long. So now, for the time being, he was relatively happy,
telling himself that the invasion could go ahead without
Mrs Gore's handsome son, and more than likely he'd
return home to his 'gold star mother' laden with medals
and obviously a hero. He spat out the wad of tobacco he
had been chewing while he had been singing (not very
well) the current popular jingle.

   To left and right the other ammunition barges followed
his lead. 'Optimists,' he said cynically, as they changed
course, too. 'The frigging blind leading the blind.' But even
as he said the words, he knew the capital ships would have
their spotter planes out soon looking for the lone barges,
recognizable now from the huge red danger flags they were
carrying. For it was now at least two hours since the assault

troops had hit the beaches, and if the battleships had been firing cover all that time, they'd soon be needing his cargo urgently.

So Al Gore allowed his mind to wander again, confident that his reponsibilities were minimal and that once he had dumped the shells, his part in what Eisenhower was calling in the leaflet given to all the troops, 'Our crusade in Europe', was finished. 'Yeah,' he said aloud to no one in particular, 'a crusade so that the kikes can make more money in the armament industry.' For everyone knew that Eisenhower was a Jew, just like the President was. Happy, content with his prejudices, Al Gore ploughed on to his death.

Breitmeyer watched the black soldiers. Not that they looked black now; most of them seemed to have turned a particularly strange shade of ash-green. Why didn't interest him. He was too concerned with his own scheme. Crazy as he was, he knew instinctively that this was the end of the line for him. If he were ever to take his revenge for all the pain and suffering the English had inflicted upon him over the last three years, it was now or never.

He looked at the piles of shells in their cardboard containers. All were armed and fused. He didn't know what kind, but it didn't matter. They would serve his purpose. He paused, suddenly bewildered. At the back of his mind a little voice asked, '*What purpose?*'

'Why,' he began, talking to himself softly as he often did, 'you know my purpose, don't you?'

But the little voice at the back of his mind gave no answer.

Breitmeyer looked puzzled momentarily: 'But you *must* know,' he persisted. 'The English have done wrong things to me . . .' His voice faltered a little: 'I know they have.' But he sounded doubtful, even to himself. He shook his head firmly, like a man trying to wake from a heavy sleep and forget his doubts. He said, 'I have to have revenge – that's the measure of it.'

Beyond the piled shells and his hiding place at the stern of the box-like barge, he saw one of the blacks raising his head mournfully over the side and, helped by a comrade, begin to heave and shake, as he vomited miserably.

A little to their right, one of the Italian co-belligerents who had been conscripted illegally into loading the shells, saw the two blacks, cried '*Mamma mia*' and began to do the same. Unfortunately he didn't manage to reach the side. Instead he vomited into the well of the barge.

'Jesus on a Crutch!' Al Gore cried in disgust. 'Ain't you guys got no shame? Spilling yer cookies like that in . . .'

Breitmeyer was no longer listening. The sudden activity in the tight barge awakened him to his own danger. The *Americano* only needed to get up from his perch at the controls and he might well notice the lone Italian lurking in the stern. It was time to take over before it was too late.

Swiftly he pulled the razor-sharp knife from the back of his belt. He knew exactly what to do. As mad as he was, he had not forgotten his years of training in this kind of sudden violent death. There were about eight of them, two Italians – they'd cause no trouble – and six American blacks, plus the man in charge of the craft. He was the most likely to cause trouble, of course, and he was armed. At his waist he had a pistol in the leather holster. It would be a task to get to the US petty officer before he could recover from his surprise at the attack and pull the pistol out. Once he had gotten rid of him, he'd take over. After the high speed motorboats he had once driven, the slow ugly barge would be child's play. For a moment his face creased in a puzzled frown. Where had he worked with motorboats, as a prisoner of war in England? He dismissed the thought as soon as it had come; he had been plagued by such strange questions for months. He didn't understand why. It was better to ignore such matters. They only unsettled him.

He stepped from his hiding place. He held the knife at his side, as a dentist does his pliers when he approaches a nervous patient to pull his tooth, so as not to frighten him. He came abreast of the two blacks, the one still leaning over the side retching miserably. He didn't hesitate. He knew exactly what to do. Expertly he slid the blade in between the third and fourth rib of the Negro holding his sick comrade. The man started. His spine straightened rigid like a taut bow. He gave a little gasp; it was a delicate small sound. But Breitmeyer knew it was the sound of impending death. He struck again. The man collapsed, dead, still holding on to his comrade with his dead hands.

Again Breitmeyer struck. The man vomiting gasped. The vomit scattered the length of the hull. Dark red blood welled up from his back. It spread across his fatigues swiftly. Still, he continued to vomit as he lay there across the stanchion. Breitmeyer's demented gaze glittered. Very neat. He'd have no trouble from the blacks when he had killed the white Yankee. Thus, he left them, the dead man clutching the one who was dying. It was a macabre tableau that pleased him for some reason . . .

Five

'**B**ridge!' Captain Kelsey yelled, then lowering his voice because he knew he was shouting because of the hours of bombardment, 'Bridge.'

'Captain . . . Guns here!'

'Fire away, Guns . . .' Kelsey grinned momentarily despite the tension of the battle. 'Cancel that remark. What's the problem, Guns?'

'We're running out of ammo, sir. Wonder if they've spotted the supply barges yet?'

'Not yet. But the Walrus' – he meant the *Warspite*'s spotter plane – 'can't be far off. It's a matter of urgency now. Just received a signal from the Admiralty. The Yanks are taking a lot of stick on their Omaha Beach. We're to move there once the re-supply has taken place. You know the Yanks? They're panicking. There's some talk of evacuating Omaha altogether. Just like Salerno. All right, Guns, keep at it. I'll keep you in the picture.' The phone went dead.

Two miles away, well clear of the beaches now, a thin mist was beginning to creep in from the sea. Like a silent grey cat it slipped over the water, gradually enveloping that great scene of sudden death and glory, as if some god on high had seen enough of man's handiwork for this day and wanted to blot it out.

But the young sub-lieutenant piloting the *Warspite*'s spotter Walrus sea-plane had no time for the possible symbolism of this June Tuesday. Instead, he cursed the mist. He knew he'd get a damn big rocket from his boss, the lieutenant commander, if he didn't find that ammo barge, so that the *Warspite* could help on Omaha Beach, before the fog settled in. So he came lower and lower, the engine ticking over just above stalling speed, while his seaman-observer scoured the grey watery waste for the first sign of the barges. Both of them knew they'd be identified by large red warning flags signalling danger. But, since the dawn assault there were abandoned craft enough down below, with khaki logs here and there which were dead bodies floating in between them. So it wasn't that easy.

'To port, sir . . . I think, sir,' the seaman-observer remarked after a while, obviously not too certain. 'There's so much stuff down there.'

The pilot understood. He nodded. He had glimpsed the shape in a break in the sea mist and indicated he was going down, saying, 'Just keep your eyes peeled, Jones. Just before we left, the commander said there are Jerry E-boats on the prowl.'

'Like the proverbial tinned tomato,' the young observer answered cheerfully, as the pilot started to take the obsolete plane down.

They cruised, still in the fog, until the pilot came to the hole. He peered down, goggles pushed to the back of his leather helmet for better vision. Yes, there it was. A slow-moving barge, packed high with crates, a large red danger flag at its stern. There were also two khaki-clad bodies hanging over the side and what looked like a third one in the well of the craft. But there were crew members. He could now see dark and white faces looking upwards. 'Poor sods look as if they've been in the wars,' he roared at Jones above the racket kicked up by the engines.

'Rather them than us, sir. With all them shells on board.'

He peered through his binoculars for a monent. 'Looks like 'em, sir. They're Yanks any road. Darkies by the look of 'em.'

The pilot made up his mind. 'All right, I'm taking her down. Radio the commander we've found her. I'm going to guide her to the *Warspite* on the surface. I'm not risking losing her in this fog. The commander would have my scalp if I did. Here goes.'

'Lawdie be praised!' one of the blacks cried fervently, waving his black hands above his head as if he were back at some revivalist prayer meeting in his native Deep South. 'They're limeys . . . it's a limey plane.'

'*Hallelujah!*' the other blacks around him joined in while the three Italians looked subdued and worried. For Italians they were unduly silent. At the tiller the petty officer with the crazy eyes looked back and snapped, 'Silence!'

The blacks cowered. They knew madness when they saw it. The man in charge forgot them. He concentrated on the task at hand, as the plane made its final run-in, the pilot feathering his engine as he came out of the fog, touched the waves with a light jerk, frothing them momentarily with his prop wash, then slowing down, the observer behind him in the open cockpit of the seaplane, waving to the crew, as if they were old friends.

At the tiller the petty officer cursed '*Idioten!*' and with his foot touched the hand grenades, already primed and fused, which lay there – just in case.

But soon it was clear that the strangers were not suspicious. Indeed, the pilot was so glad that he had found the barge with its all-important cargo that he took his hands off the joystick and waved too. Already he was imagining that he might be mentioned in dispatches, at least, for finding the barge. That would please Mummy back in Bognor Regis very much.

Next to him, Jones seized the loud-hailer, while the

pilot fought the controls to prevent the plane from hitting the side of the barge; something for which the young observer was grateful. After all, the barge was probably carrying enough high explosive shells to send them all to Kingdom Come – and then some. 'Ahoy there,' he called somewhat self-consciously; he was only an able seaman and now he sounded a bit like Captain Kelsey himself: '*Warspite* here. Are you our supply boat?'

The petty officer caught his breath with an audible gasp. It was as if someone had just given him a sudden vicious punch in the guts. '*Warspite*?' he heard himself stutter, hardly daring to believe his own ears. After all these years – *that* ship. It was hardly conceivable, now that he could do something to pay them back for all the suffering they had inflicted upon him over the years, that God had given him the *Warspite*.

'Do you read me?' the young seaman was calling. 'We shall lead you to our ship . . . Do you read me, coxswain?'

'Yes . . . yes,' he found himself shouting in answer, limiting himself so that they didn't notice his accent. 'I follow.'

Jones lowered his loud-hailer. 'Seems to have got the picture, sir,' he said to the young pilot. 'They seem all to be Yanks. The fellow at the controls sounds like a Yank.'

The pilot agreed. 'I can never understand them myself, although they're supposed to speak English like we do . . . Well, let's get on with it. It's going to be bloody slow the way that tin box moves. Ah well, let's get the show on the road. Let's pray we don't bump into one of those ruddy Jerry E-boats.' Concentrating on the controls, he started to turn and taxi eastwards. Behind him the barge started to follow. The stage was set, the actors were in place, the drama could commence . . .

*   *   *

The Spitfire had gone now. For a while Hawkins had heard the reassuring, if muted, whine of its Rolls-Royce engine above him in the sudden fog, but then it had vanished – perhaps the pilot had given up on the lone barge, shrouded by mist below. But he'd gone and now Hawkins knew he had to steer a course back to England on his own. He could do; he was sure of that. All the same, if another E-boat came racing in from the mist, his goose would be cooked. But he realized he couldn't tell his cargo of young GIs that. They were filling their britches as it was – they'd even forgotten to be sea-sick. So now he addressed them, knowing that if he gave them something to do, it would ease the strain, take their minds off their inherent danger. For now it must seem to them that they were the only craft left of that great armada that had set out so confidently this Tuesday morning. Swiftly, then, he told them they had to post lookouts. If they spotted anything that looked like an attacker, they were to open up with the two light machine guns they had at their disposal. 'And it wouldn't hurt if you fellows with the automatic rifles joined in as well. Frighten the bugger off – that's the trick.'

The decision appealed to them, he could see that. They set to work among themselves, lining the steel sides of the ugly craft as if they were pioneer settlers, forming a circle with their prairie schooners, waiting for the pesky redskins to come whooping in on their ponies to attack. Like excited schoolkids, playing at cowboys and Indians, they placed their packs in front of them as a kind of defensive wall and lined up spare clips of ammunition, chattering all the while among themselves. Abruptly they were no longer fearful. Suddenly this had become the big adventure and they were all Randolph Scotts (who, Hawkins had heard, was a pansy anyway), ready to save the grateful pioneer ladies from a fate worse than death.

Ruefully Hawkins shook his head. He told himself that if he had given the same order to a bunch of hairy-assed old British sweats, his answer would have been a wet raspberry and an invitation to do something anatomically impossible to himself *toot sweet*! But then they were Yanks and, good lads that the Americans were, they were inclined not to be of this world.

He dismissed the Yanks and got on with his self-imposed task, wishing he had a proper compass to steer with and that the bloody fog would go away. Still, he didn't and it wouldn't, so he had to make the best of things as they were. But as the landing barge ploughed on through the fog, he started to become aware of the hollow boom of heavy artillery, muted a little by the damp mist. But muted as it was, Hawkins' trained gunner's ear could make out it wasn't the firing of a German 88mm or 105mm – there'd be no mistaking the sharp whiplash crack and bark of the Jerry guns. This was that old familiar frightened hiss and whoosh of the biggest gun in the British Royal Navy. Somewhere out there someone was shooting a turret of 15-inch guns!

His heart leapt. He knew through the various buzzes of the last few days before D-Day that the old *Warspite* was still in the Channel. He didn't need a crystal ball to guess that she would be carrying out her old function of this last year or so, ever since there had been no enemy capital ships left to sink: she'd be supporting the beach landings. Suddenly, for some reason he couldn't fathom at the time, he knew he had to head to the sound of the firing and find out if it really were the Old Lady out there somewhere in the fog. He knew the *Warspite* couldn't possibly need him and his tin box full of frightened Yankee infantrymen. Probably he'd only be in the bloody way. All the same, he knew too, he was going to find the *Warspite*, come what may . . .

*   *   *

'Heaven arse and cloudburst!' Breitmeyer cursed in the German of his youth.

As the Walrus led him ever closer to the little plane's parent ship, his rage increased by leaps and bounds. Standing there at the controls, while in the stern the bewildered crew of blacks and Italians cowered in fear, his red-rimmed eyes blazed with barely controlled anger. Now and again he crooned crazy threats to himself, the saliva drooling from the sides of his contorted, wet lips. When the Italians heard him, they crossed themselves hastily, their dark eyes liquid with fear. After all, at his feet there were enough grenades to blow all of them to hell.

Now, as he heard the boom of the *Warspite*'s guns, Breitmeyer's madness seemed to increase. He knew he would have to sacrifice himself to realize his half-baked plan. But that didn't matter. He didn't want to live anyway. What was life to him? All that counted now was revenge. Once, as a cadet in the Royal Italian Navy, he had dreamed of great battles, with gallant officers sailing to their deaths with their flags flying and the bugles shrilling, knowing that in the manner of their death they would bring about victory.

But by the fifth year of war, he knew that was not for him, a poor crazy cripple. He wouldn't go down in history. But it didn't matter now. What mattered was that he paid them, the arrogant Anglo-Saxons, back for what they had done to him. That would be his revenge What was it the Sicilians said? Revenge is a dish that must be eaten cold and slowly. Well, that would be satisfaction enough for him. The *Warspite* must now think that it's all over. Victory was within sight. Now she and her English pigs of a crew were in for a surprise. In the moment of victory they would die. '*Porco di Madona!*' He cried the oath aloud. That would be a fine dish to eat in these last moments of his life.

It was about then that the young pilot of the Walrus

signalled through his loud-hailer that they were approaching the *Warspite*, which was somewhere behind the bank of milky white fog to the landing barge's front. He waved when he saw Breitmeyer had understood and then cried, 'We're off now! Best of luck for the trip back home!' And with that he switched off the loud-hailer and concentrated on his controls. Breitmeyer, as mad as he was, forced himself to wave. It was expected of him. The English, with their damned hypocritical smiles, were always so superficially polite to one another, but it didn't mean a thing. Now he was glad to see the back of the seaplane, as the pilot revved the engine and then started his ascent, racing across the sea in a high wake of white water to begin to climb slowly. A few moments later he was airborne and disappearing into the fog.

Breitmeyer forgot the plane. The Tommy had served his purpose. Now he strained his eyes to catch the first glimpse of that hated ship which had ruined his life . . .

The wallowing motion of Hawkins' craft increased. He knew why. He was beginning to hit the wake of the great ship somewhere ahead of him in the fog. Now the firing had ceased, but the sudden turbulence told him she was still there, probably hidden by the next fog bank.

But there were other things in the water now besides the increasing ripples of the wavelets. A shattered landing craft, listing heavily to port, came out of the mist. Around it there were the dead. They were still floating, held on the surface by their rubber lifebelts. Most of them had their faces and legs under the water, but with their rumps on the surface, looking absurd even in death. Lining the steel walls of the craft, the young GIs, a minute before chattering away excitedly, fell grim and silent in the presence of so much death.

For a moment or two, Hawkins, who was only a few

years older than they, enjoyed their discomfort. Young as he was, he had seen much of death. Now let these Yanks, so full of themselves, all that 'piss and vinegar', as they had remarked of them in the old days aboard the *Warspite*, see what life – or death – was about. They had left the safety of their huge country for 'little ole Europe' and were finding out now that the old continent wasn't so cosy and cute as they had imagined it to be. The Old World killed!

It was thus, with the landing craft nosing its way through the dead bodies, his mind full of such thoughts, that he saw the other landing craft, almost when it was too late to avoid a collision. At the very last moment, he wrenched the wheel to one side and missed her steel hull by what seemed inches. But as he cursed and felt his skinny body suddenly break out in a cold sweat, he spotted the white painted number on the other barge's side. *LC 104*. It was the barge that the Yank Al Gore had been scheduled to take the troops to Normandy in with them before O'Flynn had detailed him for some sort of special duty.

He wiped the sweat off his brow and stared at the other craft as it plodded on, wreathed already in the grey soft tendrils of the fog, virtually noiseless and without any apparent life like some latterday *Flying Dutchman*. For a moment, Hawkins was at a loss about what to do. Why was Al Gore so far off course? He was an experienced petty officer and navigator. Besides, this was only the Channel and not the breadth of the Atlantic Ocean or something.

He reached for his glasses and focused on the dark shape at the wheel, enclosed in the steel shell of the barge. It was difficult even to make out the figure, using the glasses. All the same, it didn't look like the Al Gore he knew. The cocky Yank, with his funny prejudices wouldn't have worn his naval cap set squarely on the top of his head. His style was rakish, the cap cocked at the back of his head in a very non-regulation manner or tilted to one side of his skull. Besides, it struck him now, as he adjusted the focus to get a better view of the man in the wavering fog, Al Gore wasn't a blond like the chap steering *LC 104* was. What the hell was going on?

Suddenly, startlingly, everything became so clear to him that he gasped with surprise. With the total revelation of a vision, he knew exactly what was going on and that knowledge filled him with a stomach-churning, frightening dread of a kind that he had never known in his young life before. In a flash, it all came together: the strange skipper in charge of a barge packed high with 15-inch shells; the fact that the lone barge way off course didn't acknowledge him, and now emerging from the fog bank some half a mile away, there was no mistaking that well-remembered dear old silhouette. It was the *Warspite*, her guns now silent, advancing upon them at slow speed!

'God Almighty!' Hawkins cried aloud, carried away by the enormity of his revelation, startling his young GIs manning the sides, 'HE'S GONNA SINK THE OLD LADY!'

Six

N ow the great old ship heaved to.

On the deck and derricks, the Fleet Air Arm mechanics and riggers prepared to take the Walrus on board as she taxied to a stop next to the *Warspite*, while other deck crews prepared to unload the new ammunition which, as the young sub-lieutenant pilot had just reported by radio, was on its way.

The crews were happy. The gun crews were virtually exhausted. They had fired over ninety shells to aid the hard-pressed Americans at Omaha and the captain had given an order which had to be unique in the three-hundred-year history of British naval gunnery: 'Fifty rounds 15-inch rapid fire!' It had been very effective. It had broken up an enemy counter-attack, but it had been exhausting for the gunners. As for the guns themselves, Guns, the senior gunnery officer, reckoned their barrels were about worn out. They'd manage to get rid of the fresh ammo now coming up in the barge. After all that was gone, it would be back to Pompey for a barrel refit.

On the bridge Captain Kelsey felt his hands shaking. It had been a nerve-racking day. Now here he was in the middle of a long-distance battle, heaved to, with all his big gun ammo gone, save the shells still in the breeches of the 15-inchers. Fortunately the fog still gave the *Warspite* some cover. But if the Hun did launch a surprise attack, he'd have a devil of a job defending the Old Lady.

He shook himself visibly and reminded himself that during this war, the *Warspite* had suffered grievous damage at the hands of the Huns four times and survived. Now she was admittedly worn out – all that damage and all those battles from the Arctic to the Med had taken their toll. But somehow he knew, as the landing barge sailed out of the fog bringing that all-important cargo, that the old ship would survive this battle too. He pursed his lips. The *Warspite* was not a pretty ship, he realized. Indeed she looked distinctively old-fashioned and perhaps a little ugly, too – after all she had been laid down before the Great War. But having said that, she *did* possess a kind of beauty of strength and character. The thousands of officers and men who had served on her – and sometimes died on her, too – had always known that.

Now the old ship was coming to the end of the road. It was a fact of life, a pensive Captain Kelsey told himself and remembered in that same instant those few lines of Wordsworth he had learned so long before at his prep school: 'Men we are and must grieve when even the shade Of that which once was great and has passed away . . .'

He smiled a little sadly at the memory and then he was businesslike again. He picked up his bridge phone and called, 'GUNS?'

'Sir?' the gunnery officer replied immediately as if he had been standing by the fire control tower phone waiting for this call all along.

'The ammo's here. Your chaps have exactly fifteen minutes. Clear?'

'Clear, sir,' Guns replied promptly. 'We'll do it.'

'I know you will,' Captain Kelsey said and put down his phone. Right up to the very end the HMS *Warspite* was going to be a damn well tight-run ship. As always, she and her crew would never let down a tradition which went back three centuries.

Suddenly content and at peace with himself after that sudden phase of uncertain despondency, he stared at the approaching barge . . .

Breitmeyer found himself breathing hard and fast, his ribcage sinking in and out hectically; it was as if he were running a great race. He knew why. It was a virtually uncontrollable excitement. Before him, towering upwards like a mighty steel cliff, lay the *Warspite* – and she was totally vulnerable. Her guns were silent and the unloading crews were waving him, seemingly controlling his approach, obviously in no way suspicious.

Breitmeyer gave that crazy lopsided smile of his, his eyes glittering, as if he were suffering from a high fever. Behind him the little crew still cowered with fear. He had warned them what would happen if they made a wrong move. A couple of the grenades, still at his feet, and they would be dead men in moments. They were heeding his warning, staring at the scene in front of them uncomprehending, but petrified with fear. He laughed curtly. They'd be dead men soon anyway, he told himself. He would be, too. But what did it matter? He would have had his revenge, and that was all that mattered.

Cautiously he revved the engine, gaze fixed on the Tommies high above him on the deck of the *Warspite*. They didn't notice the change in speed. That was important. The grinning English monkeys with their caps at the backs of their heads would find out only when it was too late. But he needed increased speed. He couldn't rely just on the grenades. The impact, however, would do the job. It would be like some monstrous torpedo slamming into the side of the enemy battleship. Even her thick armour plate wouldn't be able to withstand the explosive shock of his cargo of 15-inch shells detonating. The *Warspite* wouldn't stand a chance. She'd go down like a brick!

He took his hand off the controls for a moment and picked up two of the grenades. They were of the Anglo-Saxon type of 'egg grenade', as they called them in German. They had a four-second fuse, once the little cotter pin was pulled. He placed them handily on the little shelf in front of him. They'd serve the purpose he intended for them.

Now they were getting ever closer. He guessed the distance separating him from the *Warspite* was perhaps a mere two hundred metres. A few more minutes and there'd be no saving her from disaster. Now he was almost within striking range. The HMS *Warspite* was almost finished . . .

The blinding white light caught him totally by surprise. One moment, Breitmeyer felt he was alone with the *Warspite*, the next the star flare exploded directly to his front, its icy white glare blinding him temporarily, as he flung up his arm to shield his eyes. 'Great crap on the Christmas tree—' he began. The words died on his cracked, parched lips. There it was. Another barge heading straight for the gap between his own landing craft and the enemy battleship.

Even as Breitmeyer realized that his dastardly plan was beginning to go wrong, a ragged volley of fire erupted the length of the strange barge's port side. Bullets plucked the water white all around the *LC 104*. In the stern, one of the Italians flung up his arms dramatically, the back of his battledress blouse suddenly a bright pink. For a moment he stood there, pawing the air, as if he were climbing the rungs of an invisible ladder. The next he pitched forward, dead before he hit the deck.

Breitmeyer opened the throttle even more. The barge was heavily laden. But it started to respond. A white bone grew at its teeth. The *Warspite* became ever larger. It seemed to fill the whole horizon now. A couple of hundred yards away, a frantic Hawkins yelled at his suddenly sweating GIs, 'Hit the bastard, will ye! What frigging kind of shots are you Yankee bastards? . . . Come on . . . come on, lads!'

They redoubled their efforts. A hail of fresh fire broke from their Garand automatic rifles. At that range, even the worst shot among them couldn't miss. The superstructure of the other landing barge was ripped to shreds. Great gleaming metal scars appeared the length of its hull. Debris came tumbling down. Blacks shrieked in terror. Here and there they couldn't stand the firing. Chancing their luck, they sprang over the side and were swallowed up by the green sea, fighting the waves valiantly, not realizing no one was going to chance his life to save them. Soon they would die as obscurely as they had lived.

Captain Kelsey recovered from his shock at this sudden outburst of wild firing between two apparently Allied vessels. He grabbed his loud-hailer. From the bridge, he yelled, 'What the devil's going on down there, First Lieutenant? In heaven's name sort it—'

The words died on his lips. The closest of the two barges, the one carrying the 15-inch shells was picking up speed mightily. 'Christ All-bloody Mighty!' he gasped with shock. 'She's going to ram us!' As if to his own unspoken command, next moment the deck guns broke into wild firing, their crews knowing that if they didn't stop the *LC 104* they had only moments to live.

Now everywhere machine guns were chattering urgently. Men were flinging themselves to the deck of the *Warspite*. Petty officers shrilled their whistles urgently. Red-faced officers bellowed orders. All was chaos and confusion.

On the deck of the *Warspite*, a Chicago Piano burst into a fury of action. A white wall of tracer erupted in front of the rogue barge. But nothing seemed able to stop it. It was dying in the water, bright metal holes punched in its steel sides everywhere, sinking by the instant. Still it came on, emerging still afloat from every fresh burst of lethal fire.

Staring down from the bridge, the Captain of the *Warspite* caught a glimpse of the barge's skipper. His hat. It was gone. Blood trickled down the side of his face. But the man didn't seem to notice. He was laughing crazily, as mad as a March hare, and in his hand he clutched what Kelsey took to be a hand grenade, lifting it to his mouth. Instinctively Kelsey knew what the man at the wheel was going to do. He was going to pull the cotter pin out of the grenade with his teeth and fling it into the back of the craft. That itself, the alarmed captain of the *Warspite* knew, wouldn't ignite the 15-inch shells piled up there, but if he managed to steer his damned landing barge into the side of the *Warspite* . . .

Kelsey daren't think that terrible thought to its logical conclusion. Instead he cried urgently, voice fervent with sudden emotion, 'Kill that man . . . Kill that man!' And even as he gave the command, he realized with a shock that he had never issued the order to kill a single individual in all his long fighting career. In five years of combat, war and sudden death had been impersonal, kept at a distance, never intent on killing single fellow human beings. It had always been the collective faceless opponent known as the 'enemy'. But now he really did want the man slaughtered who was trying to sink his beautiful Old Lady at the moment of her greatest triumph . . .

It was the same thought that motivated Petty Officer Jim Hawkins, as he realized that if he didn't do something in the next few minutes all would be lost. The *Warspite* would never be able to get out of the way of the landing barge packed with high explosive shells. She'd be rammed. There'd be no saving her then. She'd go down like a stone. '*Never!*' he cried fiercely. Now there was only one course left open. 'Overboard,' he cried . . . Overboard, you soldiers!'

Flushed excited young American faces flashed round. They stared at him in wonder. 'What d'ya mean—'

'OVER THE SIDE!' he screamed in a frenzy of fury. 'Get yourselves over . . . while you've still got a chance . . . I'M GOING TO RAM HER!'

That did it. A few hesitated. The majority didn't. Tossing aside their rifles and ripping off their helmets, they scrambled over the side of the racing barge and hit the water, gasping and spluttering with its coldness as they fell behind in the barge's foaming white wake.

Hawkins dismissed them. They didn't matter. He didn't either. All that mattered now, as the shattered wreck of *LC 104*, very low in the water, kept on with a grim and terrible purpose for its date with destiny, was to destroy her before it was too late . . .

LC 104 was an indescribable mess. She was knee-deep in water and more was rushing in relentlessly from a dozen holes in her hull. Everywhere there was grotesquely twisted metal and the debris of the mess-tins of duty-free cigarettes, brooms, a few bottles and the dead themselves, black and white. They lay there, soaked and wan, sprawled out extravagantly, occasionally screwed in tight balls, but all had hands pressed, white-knuckled in death, tightly to their ears, as if to cut out the noise. Now the noise was cut out for ever.

Breitmeyer, bleeding badly now from the wound in his forehead, occasionally half-blinded by it, heard and saw nothing. All his attention, now in his dying frenzies, was concentrated on that sheer steel cliff towering high above him. He was getting closer to it by the instant. Even blinded as he was now and again, he could see her every rivet, the oil-stained leaks, the rusty lower plates. He chuckled.

It wasn't a pleasant sound. But the laughter of the stark raving mad is never pleasant.

He had tossed the grenade over the side. He wouldn't need it now. He had all the speed he needed to ignite the shells. Again he laughed crazily, ignoring the burst of heavy machine guns' bullets which ripped the length of his front. He hung on, fighting a sudden red mist which for some reason or other had appeared out of nowhere and was threatening to overcome him.

'Go away,' Breitmeyer snarled, his face wolfish now. He waved his hand in front of his face to make the mist go away. But it persisted. He forgot it. He had enough to do to keep the sinking barge on course.

A burst of fire caught him like a blow from a giant fist. It ripped the length of his guts. His entrails slipped out of the sudden red gore like a steaming grey snake. He couldn't remove his hand from the controls to tuck them back in again. So he let them fall to the deck, to lie pulsating there as if they had a separate life of their own.

He was weakening badly now. Some memory of his youth in the high meadows, perhaps of his native Tyrol, swept into his crazy fading mind and he spoke in the almost forgotten dialect of his boyhood to the gentle brown cows with the tinkling bells and the evergreen garlands around their necks. But that boyhood scene swept out again as swiftly as it had entered and the weary smile which softened fleetingly his hard demented face vanished.

Then it happened. Out of the corner of his eye, he caught a brief glimpse of that flurry of white water. A great blow struck the side of the *LC 104*. He saw a body sailing through the air from the barge which had struck him. Next moment it vanished into the wake. For an instant nothing happened.

Abruptly he found himself on his knees, gasping for breath frantically, like a boxer fighting a count of ten. With the last of his strength he fought off the final opponent. His head bent. His blood splattered the deck in bright red gobs. He tried to raise his head. It was like trying to lift a tremendous weight. He couldn't do it. He gave up.

For a moment or two he lingered there, head bent to fate in final supplication. What might have been a smile played about his bloodless lips briefly. Next instant he died, slipping silently to the deck. A moment later the *LC 104* exploded with a tremendous roar.

Gasping and spluttering in the icy water some hundred yards away, Jim Hawkins felt his face buffeted back and forth by the impact of that great explosion. Then his eyes closed and he knew no more.

Majestically the Old Lady, her hull riddled with silver scars from that last explosion, sailed on, the last of her proud line; sailed on into the grey mist of history . . .

ENVOI

First Entry In Warspite's Ship's Book

The Ship's Book contains particulars regarding the ship from the date when she was ordered to be built till finally removed from the Navy List.

Admiralty instructions on flyleaf of the Seventh Warspite*'s Ship's Book*

Last Entry

Final Disposal of Ship.
Approved to scrap, July 31, 1946.
(S.M.B.A. 2671/46)

By Mr J. Hawkins, D.C.M., Chief Gunner's Mate
HMS *Warspite*, 1938–43

In May 1954, I was on holiday with my wife in Cornwall. It was there that we heard the bad news. The old *Warspite* had run aground on the beach at Mounts Bay. We were down there like greased lightning – and we weren't the only ones. There were loads of matelots who had served on the Old Lady, even blokes who had fought with her at Jutland back in 1916.

It was heartbreaking. We could get within a few yards of her at low tide and watch the shipbreakers going to work on her – they weren't too popular with me and my shipmates, I can tell you. They were busy cutting her to pieces with their torches and the cranes were lifting bits of rusting steel into the lighters and there were DUKWS going back and forth between the two halves of her on the beach. In the end, half of us matelots who had served on her were in tears blubbing away like a ruddy lot of snotty-nosed kids.

I know why. Because we remembered her like she'd been back in peacetime – all spotless teak decks, her brasswork flashing in the sun, her gun muzzles burnished till you could see your face in them. Me, I thought of her during the war as well, when Old ABC had flown his flag in her: her sides rusting and the white teak painted over, but with her guns as well kept as ever – and always pointed in the direction of the enemy.

But then the next day it was announced that the Old Lady had been sold to a Bristol firm of scrap merchants and that did it. We'd had enough. Later, I heard that her hull had been flogged to the Wolverhampton Metal Company for a few thousand quid and what was left of the seventh *Warspite* was pulled to pieces by Brummie workmen. Funny, in a way, our own people did what the Eyeties and the Jerries couldn't do in two world wars. We're a funny race . . .